NO ANGEL

A NO SHAME HOLIDAY ROMANCE

NORA PHOENIX

No Angel (A No Shame Holiday Romance) by Nora Phoenix

PUBLISHER'S NOTE

1

The kitchen hummed with activity, delicious smells wafting from the open oven. Josh did a last check on the turkey, and when he confirmed it was perfectly cooked, he carefully lifted it out of the oven.

"T minus fifteen," he told Indy, who stuck a fork into the potatoes to see if they were done.

"Good. We're right on schedule," Indy said, sending him a happy smile.

Josh took off the oven mitts and put them back into the drawer. The turkey could rest now before their dinner commenced. He checked his list to make sure they hadn't forgotten anything. Indy was making the mashed potatoes, the water for the green beans simmered at a low boil, a sweet potato casserole was browning in the other oven, so it looked like everything was going smoothly.

Behind him, Charlie and Brad were setting the table, with Charlie gently providing instructions. Josh smiled at his patient correction whenever Brad got something wrong. Brad's dog, Max, napped in the kitchen's corner, having discovered that's where the best snacks were coming from.

Meanwhile, Blake and Aaron had retreated to the playroom. Blake had apologized, since Aaron was supposed to help with cooking, but he'd had a rough few days at work, apparently. Blake had asked if they could utilize the room for an hour or two so they could play and let Aaron regroup. Of course, they'd all assured them that was fine.

From the living room, sounds of the football game on TV drifted in, with Noah, Connor, and Miles commenting on what sounded like a close match. It was a good thing the Patriots weren't playing, since Miles was a staunch Seahawks fan and liked to goad Noah and Connor about their love for all things Patriots. It was all done in good fun, though Miles liked to live dangerously at times, riding Connor hard.

"The potatoes are done," Indy said.

Josh opened the can of cranberry sauce and dumped it into a bowl. He'd wanted to make it himself but had been overruled by a majority that store-bought was fine, if not better. It went somewhat against his preference for home-cooked food, but he had acquiesced.

"I've put out all the ingredients for your mashed potatoes," he told Indy.

Watching Indy cook was always fun. He'd gotten much better at it, but it still required a lot of focus and concentration from him. Josh watched, his heart softening, as Indy added sour cream and some fresh chives to the bowl and turned the mixer on, the tip of his tongue peeping out from between his lips.

"I love you."

Those words kept falling off his lips all by themselves, and they never failed to make Indy shine with joy at hearing them. Even now, concentrated on getting the mashed potatoes right, he stopped the mixer for a few seconds to face

Josh and send him a look so full of love it took Josh's breath away.

"I love you too."

Would he ever grow tired of hearing those words, either from Indy or from Connor? Josh doubted it. Every time he thought his heart couldn't get any fuller, it seemed to make more space. And two days from now, he'd make it official by marrying Connor. It would be a small affair, their double wedding, but that didn't make it less meaningful. On the contrary, it had always been about their love, not about others or throwing a party. Their wedding fit their love, their family, their hearts.

As Indy went back to his cooking and Josh checked the casserole in the oven, he pondered it. The heart was a funny thing, wasn't it? The older he got, the more he realized that so many people got things wrong about love. He himself had grown up with such a warped version of love, his parents only loving him as long as he conformed to their standards, to their norms. How wrong they had been to call that love.

Love couldn't have conditions, Josh had realized. Love possessed no limits, no fear, no shame. Love rose above that; otherwise, it wouldn't be love. If nothing else, the past year had taught him that. The love that reigned in this house, it wasn't traditional by any standard.

God, his parents would have a fucking heart attack if they ever found out he was in love with not one, but two men. Then Josh thought of their reaction if they ever discovered their other son, Aaron, was not only madly in love with a man as well but got off on pretending to be a puppy with that same man as his owner. They wouldn't just have a heart attack, they would legit die. Either of embarrassment or shame—Josh wasn't sure which—but it was their problem.

No one who had ever seen Blake and Aaron together could deny how happy and perfect they were for each other.

And the same was true for Miles and his boys, another unconventional relationship. Josh had not only seen it work, but flourish. He'd had his doubts in the beginning, not because he questioned the love between the three men, but because of the unusual dynamics. Miles being a daddy to Brad, but not to Charlie, and Charlie being way more of a bossy little shit than any of them had expected, and yet it worked. They fit together, like a seamless puzzle.

"Josh, baby, are you with me?" Indy asked, and Josh realized he'd been staring into space for a while. No wonder Indy was checking if he wasn't having an episode.

He turned toward him. "I'm good, just...thinking."

Indy studied him for a few seconds more, then smiled. "There is a lot to be grateful for, isn't there?" he asked, showing once again he could read Josh's mind.

Josh nodded. "There is. I can't help but think how lucky and blessed we are with our chosen family."

"We are. It hits me on days like this as well," Indy said, and they shared another moment before they went back to cooking.

Indy set the mashed potatoes aside as Josh added the green beans to the boiling water. He'd prepared a nice dressing for them made with nut oil, lemon juice, and pecans and goat cheese. By the time everything was done, Josh beamed with pride because it all looked amazing. And the timing was dead-on.

They arranged all the food on the beautifully set table and called in the others. Aaron's previous haunted look had been replaced by the inner peace he often radiated after a puppy play session, and Josh gave him a quick hug. "Feeling better?"

"Much," Aaron said, hugging him back. "Blake always knows how to center me."

"Good. You needed it," Josh said as he let go of his brother.

"The table looks amazing," Miles said, pride audible in his voice. "You boys did a terrific job."

Brad's face lit up. "That was all Charlie, but thank you, Daddy. I helped."

Miles pressed a tender kiss on his lips. "I know you did, sweetheart. Thank you for listening to Charlie's instructions. You did really well."

Charlie had created name cards for everyone. Handcrafted, beautifully written cards with hand-painted leaves on them. The leaves matched the ones on the napkins Charlie had picked out and folded into intricate flowers. It was a little over the top for an informal gathering like this and yet it was perfect. It was one of the things that Josh loved, how they all had started to explore unique talents and interests.

They found their usual spots, he and Indy next to each other, with Connor and Noah flanking them on either side, and Miles and his boys on either side of him across from them. Blake and Aaron were sitting next to them, with Blake sitting next to his younger brother. Josh was happy to see the two of them growing much closer over the last few months. After some initial struggles, Blake had adapted wonderfully to Brad's unique relationship with Miles, and he fully supported it. Not that Josh had expected anything else from a man who loved to engage in puppy play, but it was beautiful to see him accept this was what Brad needed.

They had just all sat down, everyone praising how beautiful both the table setting and the food looked, when the doorbell rang. Max raised his head and barked, then plopped down again. Josh tensed up. Someone dropping by unexpectedly on Thanksgiving Day? That couldn't be good.

Connor's hand gripped his neck instantly, and Indy reached for his hand from the other side. "We've got you, baby," Connor's calm voice said. "Just breathe, I'll check it out."

Josh was grateful that Connor waited till Josh was okay before he rose from his chair and hurried to the front door. After he'd opened it, a faint conversation was audible, but not loud enough for Josh to recognize the other voice.

Then Connor called out, "Blake and Brad, can you come over for a second? Your brother is here."

BLAKE SHARED a stunned look with Brad. Burke was here? When he and Aaron had visited his younger brother, Benjamin, earlier that morning, Benjamin had mentioned something about Burke calling him and telling him he would visit. Blake hadn't known what to make of that, had thought maybe Benjamin had gotten confused. After all, none of them had heard a peep from Burke since he'd stormed out of this house months ago.

His first instinct was to face Burke alone, but then he realized he couldn't and shouldn't make that decision for Brad. He'd made that mistake too many times in the past, deciding for Brad rather than allowing him to make his own decisions.

So he asked, "Do you want me to talk to him first, or would you prefer facing him together?"

Much to his surprise, Brad didn't look to Miles for guidance. "You talk to him first. If he's still set on being an asshole, I'd much prefer not to see him."

As harsh as that sounded, Blake couldn't agree more with him that it was for the best. He was still amazed at the change in Brad compared to a year ago. The relationship with Miles and Charlie, the guidance he got from the daddy dynamic, it was nothing short of amazing. He'd lost his default sullen expression and, even though he still struggled at times, there was a new joy and contentment in him. No need to let Burke take that from him if he—as Brad had worded it so perfectly—was still set on being an asshole.

He put a soft hand on his brother's shoulder. "I'll go see what he wants."

He made his way to the front door, where Connor had let Burke in, but not beyond the entrance. Blake appreciated that the man was looking out for all of their best interest, but especially Brad's. Connor was a stand-in daddy when Miles was away, Blake knew, and Brad treated Connor with nothing but respect and admiration.

Blake shot him a look of gratitude. "Thank you. I've got this."

With one last, none-to-friendly glance at Burke, Connor went back to the kitchen. Blake studied his brother. He looked well, a little more tan than before, and from the looks of it, well-rested and fed.

"What brings you here?" he asked.

Burke met his inquisitive gaze head on. "I thought it was a good day to make amends, but I apologize for intruding. I tried your house first, but your current house guests said you were celebrating Thanksgiving here, so I came over before I lost the nerve."

"The nerve for what?"

"To apologize for being a complete asshole to you."

Blake cocked his head, then studied his brother a little more. "There's something different about you," he observed.

Burke smiled, but it wasn't a happy smile. "Maybe because I'm sober?"

Blake couldn't help his eyes from widening. "Sober?" he repeated stupidly, his mind contemplating what Burke meant. Their father had been an alcoholic, a mean one, and surely Burke wouldn't be stupid enough to fall into the same addiction, would he?

"Apparently, I managed to hide it well, but I've been a high-functioning alcoholic for the last few years. After I ran off from you, I quit my job and moved down South, looking for a fresh start. I thought a change of scenery would help me, and it did, but not until after I hit rock bottom. But that's a story for another day. I just wanted to tell you I'm sober and that I want to make amends."

Blake blinked slowly. "You're going through the program," he said, recognizing Burke's language. Holy fuck, his brother was an alcoholic. "The steps. You're following the steps." He knew them well enough from the many people who'd stayed in his house who'd been recovering drug or alcohol addicts, fueled by their years of being abused.

Burke hesitated, but then he nodded. "Yes, but that's not why I'm apologizing. It's not because it's a requirement or a step. I mean it. I fucked up big time with you."

Burke was an alcoholic. How the hell had he missed that, Blake wondered. He was hit with a similar sense of anger at himself as when he'd discovered Brad's issues. He'd always thought he'd been close with his brothers. How wrong he had been. Brad had suffered so hard, and Blake had never noticed enough to say anything, and here was Burke, admitting to a years-long addiction Blake had known nothing about. But he would have to deal with that later.

This wasn't about him or his failures. This had to be about Burke.

"I appreciate you coming and apologizing," Blake said. "I hope you realize we'll need some more conversations before I can put this behind us, but you coming here is a great start."

He watched as Burke visibly relaxed a little, then said, "You didn't hurt only me, though. The fact that you ran off from Brad as well impacted him. He's been going through a lot of stuff, and he could've used your support."

"Is he okay? The cancer isn't back, is it?" Burke asked, a hint of panic in his voice. Somehow, that made Blake feel better. Despite all his shortcomings, Burke really did care about them.

"Physically, he's fine. Emotionally, he's been dealing with a lot, but he's got it handled now, or at least, he's getting there." He waited a beat to consider how much he should tell Burke, then decided he'd better test the waters as promised. "He's seeing someone. It's serious."

Burke's eyes widened. "Brad's got a boyfriend?"

"He's got two: Miles—the FBI agent who protected Indy for a while—and Charlie, who you know. The three of them are in a committed relationship. Moreover, Miles and Brad have a daddy–boy relationship. I'm telling you all this before I allow you to come in further. This is not my house, but Brad does live here, and I won't allow you to criticize him, his relationship, or that of the other people present. That includes Aaron, by the way, and yes, he and I are still engaged in puppy play. Is any of this going to be an issue for you?"

He realized it was somewhat cruel of him to stack all this information and dump it on Burke like this. But he had to know what his brother's attitude would be like. In this house, he couldn't let him in if he was set on continuing the judgmental behavior he had shown before toward Blake and Aaron. That wouldn't fly here, and Blake would do whatever it took to not only protect his brother, but his boyfriend and everyone else.

Burke swallowed, his Adam's apple bobbing. "That's..." He cleared his throat, then tried again. "That's all fine. I won't say anything. It doesn't mean much, but I am awfully sorry about the way I treated Aaron, and your relationship. I'd love the opportunity to explain why I reacted like that in more detail, but another time."

Blake saw nothing but honesty on his brother's face, then questioned if he even knew him well enough to make that judgment. "Understand this: you know I'm a man of second chances. I always have been. But where the people in this house are concerned, you'll find the second chance is your last one. This is family, Burke, and I'm telling you to respect that. You fuck up again, and you're out. I don't care if you're my brother by blood, I will not allow you to hurt those I love again. Do you understand me?"

Burke blinked a few times. "You've changed," he said. "I've never seen you this protective."

"Well, we've all changed. Brad, me, and hopefully you. Brad and I have changed for the better, and I hope that's the case with you as well."

Burke cringed a little. "I'd love to say yes, but I'm much too aware I'm very much a work in progress, so I hope you cut me some slack as I try to rediscover myself."

"Slack, yes, but I've told you where I draw the line. As long as you stay on the right side of that line, we're good. You want to come in to celebrate Thanksgiving with us?"

"Are you sure I'm welcome?" Burke asked. "I'm not sure what you told everyone, but I can't imagine I'm high on their list of people they would like to have over for a family holiday like this."

For the first time, Blake sent him a genuine smile, and he put a hand on Burke's shoulder as he spoke. "Bro, you'll find there's not a more welcoming bunch than these people. They will take you in as one of their own if you'll accept them as they are."

A little frown appeared between Burke's eyes. "Are you telling me the puppy play and daddy kink isn't all of it?"

Blake laughed. "Dude, not even half."

2

B rad couldn't believe Burke had shown up like that. Blake had brought him into the living room and had told him to wait there, then had gestured Brad to come over for a quick chat. He'd done it in private, just the two of them, telling him that Burke had apologized and was serious about making amends. He'd asked Brad if he was okay with Burke staying. Of course, Brad had said yes. It was Thanksgiving, for fuck's sake. How could you say no on a day like this?

But no matter what Burke had told Blake, Brad wasn't sold just yet. So far, his brother had kept quiet, seemingly content to observe while the others talked. That wasn't unusual, as all the Kent brothers were introverts, but Brad kept waiting for him to speak up and say something stupid. Or mean. Or judgmental.

He didn't like it, Burke being there, not one bit. This was his home, his safe space, and yet here was a man who had judged Blake and Aaron for their puppy play. What were the odds of him being on board with the rest of the kink that was so prevalent in this house? Obviously, Brad's own relationship with Miles and Charlie was first and foremost on his mind.

Blake had assured Brad that he'd laid down the law for Burke and that Burke had said he was okay with it. He'd told him about the daddy stuff and everything, Brad had concluded. But knowing it and agreeing to it in theory wasn't the same as watching it, seeing it played out before your eyes.

So far—and Burke had been here for about thirty minutes now—Brad had managed to behave so well that Miles hadn't needed to admonish him. Sure, he'd called Brad *boy* a time or two, but that was a hell of a lot more subtle than some of the other stuff that came up on a regular basis. How would Burke react to that?

The thought put Brad's stomach in uncomfortable twists, and he poked around at the green beans on his plate. He shouldn't hate it, his own brother showing up, but he did, because it threatened to disturb his sense of being safe, of being home that he relished so much.

"Stop playing with your food," Miles told him, his tone still mild, but Brad spotted the writing on the wall.

"I'm not hungry," he said, barely avoiding tacking on that *Daddy* he'd become so accustomed to.

Miles's raised eyebrow told him his daddy had noticed that deliberate omission. Under the table, Miles's hand traveled to Brad's thigh, and he got a little warning squeeze. That was Miles's subtle signal that Brad should behave.

He closed his eyes, so conflicted about what to do. What if Burke laughed at him? Made fun of him? What if he displayed that same judgmental asshole attitude he'd shown to Blake and Aaron? Brad had been too scared to say something back then, too uncertain of his own position. Would he have the guts right now to say something?

Miles squeezed his thigh again, and somehow, it brought a new thought to Brad's head. He wouldn't have to. This time, he wouldn't have to stand up to Burke by himself. Blake would have his back, and he damn well knew Miles would. Hell, Charlie could be a little firecracker if somebody hurt Brad, and he would stake all his money on even Connor and the others speaking up for him.

A wave of emotion rolled through him as he realized that this was his *home*. Burke was the stranger here, the intruder. Brad had home advantage, and his family wouldn't let him down.

He raised his chin and defiantly looked at Burke as he spoke. "Sorry, Daddy. I was a little distracted. I promise I'll eat my beans."

"That's my good boy," Miles said, and his hand left Brad's thigh to rub his hair. "I'm so proud of you, sweetheart."

Brad knew his daddy wasn't talking about eating those damn beans, though they were far from Brad's favorite food. No, Daddy knew the courage it had taken him to take this stand, and Brad lifted his head even higher. Burke had jerked at the word "daddy," but now he looked up and met Brad's eyes. There was no judgment there, just confusion, as far as Brad could tell. He could live with that, he decided. Max rubbed against his legs, then dropped to the floor underneath Brad's chair, and Brad fed him some beans while no one looked.

Despite Burke's presence, conversation flowed during the meal, with Charlie recounting some fantastic tales of clients he'd encountered. He'd gotten involved with a national group of drag queens as their personal make-up artist, and he loved it. He was taking classes in makeup or something as well, and he loved to experiment on Aaron.

Hell, he'd even tried stuff on Brad, who had willingly sat

down and let Charlie play with him for close to two hours. Sure, Charlie had promised him a sex fest afterward, and there was little Brad wouldn't do for that, but he could admit it had been fun to see himself transformed into someone else.

"Before we bring out the desserts, Indy and I thought it would be a great idea to do the traditional Thanksgiving thing and share what we're grateful for," Josh said. "I know it's a little cliché, but while cooking, we realized how much has changed for all of us and how grateful we are to be here together on this day, so it seems fitting."

Noah nodded, sending Indy a look stuffed with love. "I think that's terrific, and I'll go first. I'm grateful that Indy is where he belongs: with all of us, but especially with Josh and me and Connor. For a long time, the future looked so bleak that I doubted this day would ever come, so..." He cleared his throat, and Brad could hear the emotion in his voice as he continued. "Yeah, that's what I'm grateful for."

"I second that," Connor spoke up. "But I'm also grateful that we're getting married in two days. I know that sounds like the thing I'm supposed to say, and obviously, I'm gonna rub it in you didn't think to mention that, Flint," he said with a laugh at Noah, who shot him a middle finger. "But the truth is that my heart has been full of little else besides the wedding. It seems like a miracle, the four of us together, preparing for such a special day."

Brad wondered if those four realized they had stopped talking about them as couples and had started to refer to themselves as a foursome. It used to be that Noah spoke of himself and Indy or Indy and Josh, and Connor had been even more consistent, always referring to the couples in their complicated relationship. But Noah had just casually linked their four names together, and now Connor had done the same. *Interesting.* What was happening there?

"That was beautiful, baby," Josh said, his eyes making starry hearts at Connor. Connor stole a quick kiss, then gestured at Burke.

"I'm... I want to thank you all for welcoming me, a stranger to most of you, to your table today. I'm grateful to be with my brothers and for the grace they're showing me," Burke said.

Damn, the man could still talk. That had always been his forte. He was good with words when he wanted to be.

"Oh gosh, I'm not good at this kind of thing. I'm grateful for so many things," Charlie said. "I'm grateful I'm safe and loved. I'm beyond grateful for my two wonderful boyfriends and for the future that awaits us. My job is fantastic, I love living here, and I love you all so very much."

It was uncharacteristically mushy for Charlie, which made it even more special to Brad. He reached in front of Miles and grabbed Charlie's hand to squeeze it.

"I love you," Charlie mouthed at him, and Brad whispered the same thing back at him with Miles sending them both a happy and proud look.

"I'm grateful for my two boys, who are the joy of my life," Miles said, kissing first Charlie on his head, then Brad. "A year ago, I couldn't have thought I'd ever be this happy and content. It's been a year of big changes, but I don't regret a single one of them. And as Charlie said, I'm so happy and grateful we have met you all."

The joy of his life. Brad had heard Miles say it before, but it hit him all over again. Despite all his issues, his bratty behavior, his acting out and exasperating Miles, his daddy still called him the joy of his life. How big a miracle was that?

His voice was soft but steady as he spoke up. "I'm grateful for the space to be myself and for the love and patience of everyone around me. Acceptance, I forgot to say acceptance. The fact that you guys love me just the way I am, that's..." His eyes filled up, and he wiped away the moisture with a quick gesture, feeling embarrassed. "Anyway, that's what I'm grateful for."

Miles, who apparently didn't give a flying fuck what both of Brad's brothers would think, pulled Brad on his lap and gave him a soft, deep kiss on his mouth that left him tingling and wanting more. "That was beautifully said, my sweet boy. I love that you feel so safe here. With us."

Brad looked up at his daddy, whose cock was already hardening under his ass. He'd have to take care of that later, and he'd damn well better remember to do that out of eyesight of both his brothers. Blake had seen him pleasure Miles a few times already and he hadn't said anything, but Brad knew he preferred not to watch.

"I love you, Daddy," Brad said. Watching Miles's face explode with joy at those words never got old. And he didn't disappoint him this time either. Love was a wondrous thing, Brad realized more and more.

"I have to second Brad," Josh said. "I'm grateful for the space we allow each other to be ourselves. It makes me proud when I see it, when I see us be more and more our true selves. And yes, baby," he turned toward Connor, "I am very much looking forward to our wedding, and that fills me with immeasurable joy. But at the end of the day, that too is proof of the acceptance we have. The fact that the four of us will be standing there, isn't that a miracle in itself?"

Brad saw some moist eyes all around the table, and it made him feel weak as jelly inside all over again. This tradition might be mushy and cheesy, but he would be lying if he didn't admit it provided him with a deep sense of joy and gratitude.

"As for me," Indy said, "I'm grateful for family. We can't choose the family were born into, as many of us at this table can attest to. Our blood family can hurt us, let us down, or even abandon us. But this family, the family we chose, the family we formed ourselves, this is a bond stronger than anything else. I know that no matter what storms life will bring, we will stand together. I don't care if others may judge us for who we are and how we choose to live our lives, because I wouldn't trade all of you for the world."

He teared up, Indy, and Josh grabbed his hand. Brad couldn't explain why, but Indy's words made him proud and sad at the same time. No, he realized, it wasn't sadness. It was fear. When Indy had spoken of the storms that life could bring, a chill had run down Brad's spine. What was he talking about? Did Indy know something the others didn't? Was he in danger all over again?

Brad let it go, or at least, he tried to, but as they ended that ritual with hugs and brought out the desserts, Brad couldn't quite silence the concerned voice inside him. He'd thought the danger was behind them, what with Charlie's crazy ex in prison and that drug gang Indy had been hunted down by either dead or in prison awaiting trial. Had he been wrong?

Indy had been right about one thing, though. Even if new storms came, they'd face them together. At one point, the thought of facing more adversity would've scared Brad shitless, but as he looked around the table, he realized that he felt different now. It was a strange sensation to know on the deepest level possible that not only was he willing to die for these men, but they would do the same for him.

He knew what Connor and Josh had done for Indy's

freedom. He was pretty sure he wasn't supposed to know, but he'd overheard Connor and Indy talk about it once. From the little snippets of their conversation he'd overheard, he had concluded that Josh had been the sharpshooter who had shot those guys in Boston. Brad had no idea how they had pulled it off, and he didn't want to know. He was certain Miles knew too, as his daddy was anything but stupid. But if Miles didn't think it was necessary to discuss it, Brad wouldn't either. He owed all of these men everything, so he would stay silent. And he would have their backs, as much as they had his.

3

How the fuck was it possible he was nervous about this? Indy wiped his clammy hands on the tight, dark-blue slacks he was wearing. Maybe that was it, he decided, these ridiculously dressy pants that made him feel like a...like a groom.

He sighed, turning sideways to study himself in the mirror. He looked good, he had to admit. Not that he'd had any doubt. Hell, between Colin and Charlie, they had the fashion advice covered. Colin, the sales guy from Macy's Aaron and Blake had recommended to advise them on their outfits, had instantly clicked with Charlie, the two of them bonding over fabrics and cuts and breast pockets that were or were not crucial.

Indy's eyes had glazed over, much like the other grooms, but boy, those two had delivered. He looked wicked hot, if he did say so himself.

"Damn, you look good," Miles said, and Indy turned around to face him.

"You think?"

Miles's face split open in a big grin as he pointed toward

his crotch, his hard dick outlined in the thin fabric of his suit pants. "That's what your ass in those pants does to me."

Indy harrumphed. "Pshah, you don't need my ass for that."

Miles shrugged. "True, but it really was your ass that did the trick." He stepped behind Indy and turned him toward the mirror. "You're gorgeous, Indy," he said, his face growing serious. "The four of you will look amazing together."

Indy's face softened and he let out a little sigh. "Thank you. I'm wicked nervous," he admitted.

"It's your wedding day. Nerves are to be expected," Miles said, ever the rational one.

Indy gave himself one last glance in the mirror, then turned to face Miles. "Maybe, but it's not wedding jitters or whatever you call those."

Miles's kind eyes rested on him. "It's hard to believe you're this happy," he said softly. "That all your nightmares are over."

Indy bit his lip. "It's stupid, right? To feel guilty for being happy?"

"Oh, Indy, you know better," Miles sighed, even as he pulled him in for a quick hug. He kissed the top of his head before he let him go. "It's not stupid. You've been through hell, and it's gonna take a while before you've adapted to the new reality."

"It's been months since Duncan died. Shouldn't I have adjusted by now?"

"There's no timeline for this, but I think it's safe to say it will take a while longer. You've been living under stressful and traumatic conditions for years. Your body and mind had gotten used to that. Those patterns will take a long time to change and be replaced by a more normal state. You still have to get used to being happy, Indy."

Indy sighed again. "It feels like I shouldn't be sad on my wedding day, you know?"

"I don't think you're sad. I think your mind is questioning your emotions, but if you tell it it's okay, you'll feel the happiness. Hell, I just saw Noah and Josh in their outfits. Trust me, once you see them, you will be happy."

Indy rose on his toes and pressed a soft kiss on Miles's cheek. "Thank you. You always know what to say."

Whatever Miles had wanted to say in response was interrupted by a loud complaint from the hallway.

"Daddy, Charlie says I have to wear this!" Brad stomped into the room, looking ten kinds of miserable in a charcoal-gray suit with a pink shirt and a darker pink tie.

Miles's eyes lit up, as they always did when one of his boys walked in, which Indy thought was the sweetest thing. "Look at you, my sweet boy, all dressed up," he praised him. "Don't you like what Charlie picked out for you? Look, it's the same outfit he and I are wearing, so we match."

Brad put a finger behind the collar of his shirt and tugged, his face dark with frustration. "It's so tight around my neck, Daddy. I feel like I can't swallow."

Indy chuckled. "Maybe you should test that," he suggested, winking at Brad.

"That's what I proposed to Charlie, but he said he didn't have time," Brad pouted, then shifted his gaze to Miles and peeked at him from under his lashes.

Indy couldn't help but laugh at the adorably hopeful expression on Brad's face. He'd become so much more centered over the last few months, but he still needed Miles something fierce. A few weeks ago, he'd had an incident at school where an angry parent had made a scene over a low grade, and he'd once again retreated into little kid mode, this time for over a day. Miles had handled it beautifully, being the loving daddy Brad had needed to recover from that.

Miles beckoned Brad with one finger, then pointed toward the floor in front of him. "We'd better make sure you can swallow, baby. I wouldn't want your *skills* to be impeded by your outfit."

"Yes, Daddy. Thank you, Daddy," Brad babbled, a happy smile on his face as he went to his knees, his hands already on Miles's zipper. "I knew you'd understand."

Indy watched with a smile as Brad whipped out that insatiable cock and had it in his mouth in under a second. The look on his face was pure bliss, even more so when Miles's fingers laced through his hair and pulled him closer, choking him on his dick.

"Miles, are you ready to go?" Charlie called from the hallway. "Where did Brad go? He was just..."

Charlie walked in, tightening his tie. He was sporting the same outfit as Miles and Brad, and Indy's heart warmed at how sweet they'd look together. Then Charlie spotted Brad on his knees and his eyes darkened.

"You little shit! I told you there was no time for a blow job," he protested, putting his hands on his hips.

Miles sent him a sheepish glance as he released Brad's head. "Was I supposed to say no when he asked me?"

Brad let go of Miles's cock and took a rasping breath, his eyes watery. "I didn't ask you," he pointed out, his voice a little hoarse. "Charlie made me promise I wouldn't ask you, and I didn't. You offered. Or you told me, whatever."

Charlie's eyes narrowed as they zoomed in on Miles. "And you really thought this was the best time for another blow job?"

Indy followed the exchange with amusement. These three were hilarious together at times.

"You're saying there's a wrong time for one?" Miles wondered, then raised his hands in surrender when Charlie looked like he'd explode any moment. "I'll make it fast, I promise."

He grabbed Brad's head again and stuffed his cock back into his mouth. "And I'll deal with you later, you little brat. You'll go to bed with one hell of a red ass tonight."

"Like that's gonna deter him," Charlie commented, but Indy saw his eyes warm at the sight of Brad sucking as if his life depended on it.

"Come here, my love," Miles said, and he reached for Charlie. When Charlie accepted his hand, he pulled him in and brought their mouths together for a deep kiss. Indy watched with tenderness as Miles climaxed into Brad's mouth, his soft moan swallowed by Charlie. "I love you so much," Miles whispered against Charlie's lips, even as Brad tucked his cock back in, still licking his lips with an expression of bliss.

With his other hand, Miles pulled Brad up and switched from one mouth to the other. "I love you too, my little brat. But you be good today, you hear me? Best behavior and no shenanigans."

Brad nuzzled against Miles's neck, his fingers lacing with Charlie's. "Yes, Daddy."

"The three of you look amazing together," Indy said.

Charlie beamed. "Thank you." He gave Miles and Brad a last kiss, then untangled from them and walked over to Indy to give him a final inspection. "You ready?"

Indy's heart jumped up all over again. Was he ready to do this?

The past months had been amazing, the four of them growing even closer than before. He loved Noah with all his heart and saw that love mirrored back to him every day,

Noah worshipping the very ground Indy walked on. Noah was his rock, his protector.

And Josh, Josh was the other half of his soul. He needed Josh as much as Josh needed him. They balanced each other out, their souls entwined in a way Indy wasn't even able to describe.

Connor's hesitations about if and how the four of them would work were completely gone now. He shared Josh with Indy with the same ease that Noah shared. Both men had come to understand how they fit, how Indy and Josh needed each other. They'd become a family, the four of them. He'd never imagined his heart could hold that much love, but it did. And today, he would make it official by taking Noah's name.

Indy Flint.

God, he liked the sound of that.

"Yeah," he said. "I'm ready."

NOAH HAD NEVER BEEN one to get emotional. It was not his nature, maybe still conditioned by the many lectures he'd received from his father as a boy. Showing tender emotions was showing weakness, the general had firmly believed. Noah disagreed, but it still didn't come naturally to him. Oh, he'd cried plenty in those dark days when it seemed Indy had been ripped from his arms forever, but other than that, it took a lot for him to tear up.

But as he watched Indy and Josh walk toward him and Connor, their hands linked and their eyes shining with love, his eyes definitely got misty. How had he gotten this lucky to find this much love, this much perfection? It humbled him every single day that Indy had chosen him. He looked cute as a button in his suit that matched Josh's to a T, the two of them linked as always. Yet it never felt to Noah as if he only had half of Indy's heart. His heart was so big, his love so deep, that there was enough to share.

They were crazy, of course, for doing the wedding outside in November, but it was what they'd all wanted. They'd put up Christmas lights all around the yard, which created a true winter wonderland, aided by the gentle flurries that drifted down. It was picture perfect, their small group of guests all showing wonder on their faces. Also, it would ensure the ceremony was blissfully short, as none of them appreciated formality and long speeches.

Indy beamed as he took up position next to Noah, his whole face shining like a beacon. Noah felt like his heart would burst with how full it was. He linked hands with him, engulfing that much smaller hand in his and squeezing gently.

They'd informed the officiant who was doing the ceremony about their special relationship, and the man hadn't batted an eye. They'd chosen him based on a recommendation from other LGBTQ couples who had sung his praises for showing true acceptance of uncommon relationships. He welcomed the four of them with a warm, welcoming smile as they stood before him with linked hands.

"Dear friends, we are blessed today to be in the presence of so much love and to affirm that love by uniting these men in marriage," he said, his rich, deep voice booming through the garden.

Noah's heart quieted as he listened to the officiant.

"I am honored to unite Noah, Indy, Josh, and Connor in marriage," the man said, linking their names together in a way that made Noah's heart swell with pride. "Let their love be a shining example that family is more than blood and that love has no shame."

Noah shared a look with Connor, and they smiled. They'd picked their officiant well. That thought was affirmed when the man walked them through their wedding vows and omitted the "forsaking all others" part. Smart choice.

Their answers were strong, their *I dos* filled with love. Noah locked eyes with Indy as he promised him everything and meant every single word. He'd spend the rest of his life proving to Indy he'd made the right choice.

"By the power vested in me by the state of New York, I pronounce you married. Husbands, you may seal your wedding vows with a kiss."

Their friends around them erupted in applause and cheers, but Noah only had eyes for his Indy. He cupped his cheeks and kissed him, a soft, tender kiss that had to convey all the words he couldn't seem to form.

"You're my everything, baby," he whispered. "I love you so damn much."

Indy kissed him back with that same tenderness. "I love you, Noah. So, so much."

Next to them, Connor and Josh were exchanging similar words, the big man's eyes suspiciously moist. Noah waited till they were done, then nudged Indy. "It's okay, go."

Indy's eyes teared up. "Are you sure?"

"It's your wedding day, baby. You belong to him as much as you belong to me."

Indy rose up to kiss him again, then turned around. Josh, always in tune with him, did the same, and Noah and Connor watched as they kissed, one of those sweet, languid kisses that made them seem like they were one and the same body. That, of course, resulted in more cheers from their guests.

They'd put up a party tent in their backyard, warming it with heaters. They hadn't planned for a long party anyway and hadn't wanted to rent a facility, knowing the kind of activities a party like this would result in. Privacy was the primary goal, and this worked perfectly. Besides, the guest list was short, all of them preferring to keep it limited to close friends and a few colleagues who were in the know and were fine with it. Josh had Aaron there, but he was the only family member present.

Noah had invited his father but had been open about what to expect, and the general had kindly declined. He'd sent his warmest wishes, though, with a generous gift in the form of a brand-new, state-of-the-art barbecue that Connor had all but drooled over. Noah understood. His father couldn't be seen at a wedding like this, and he didn't blame him. Their relationship had gotten better and his father had met Indy, but they would never become truly close. He could live with that.

And Connor had debated inviting his mom, he'd told them, but had decided against it. He hadn't seen her since he'd left the Marines, not wanting to be associated with his family in any way. It made things easier, in some ways, though a tad sad as well, Noah felt.

After cutting the wedding cake, it was time for the first dance, and Noah and Connor shared a look. They'd talked about this and had both agreed this was how they wanted it, but how would Indy and Josh react? Charlie put on the music they'd picked, and as the first notes of "A Thousand Years" sounded, Indy and Josh took their places with Noah and Connor, as they thought was the plan. But a few notes in, Noah and Connor both stepped back.

"This is your dance," Connor said to Josh, gesturing at Indy, and you could hear the emotion in his voice. "Your moment to shine together."

"Connor..." Josh said, his face showing conflicted emotions.

"I love you, Josh. So fucking much. Now, go dance with Indy."

Josh's face lit up. "Yes, Connor."

Indy was in his arms instantly, and those two plastered their bodies together, swaying to the music. That left Noah and Connor, who had agreed beforehand, but were now faced with the slightly awkward reality. And because he understood how hard this was for Connor, Noah bowed slightly and extended his hand.

"Lead the way, O'Connor," he said with a wink, and Connor shot him a grateful look before accepting. His strong hand laced with Noah's, and Noah pressed close against that big body, content to let the other man lead.

Noah had expected it to feel weird, dancing with Connor, but it wasn't. The man's massive body was a sharp contrast to Indy, who was usually in Noah's embrace, and yet it felt familiar. They sure as fuck had spent enough time around each other, both dressed and in various stages of undress. Connor still loved it when people watched as he fucked Josh, and Noah was happy to oblige. Hell, those live porn shows never failed to inspire him and Indy.

And they sure got their fill of those, as Miles and his boys provided regular entertainment as well. Noah was grateful for the way those three had made the ranch their home, Miles especially. In the beginning, he'd still felt embarrassed about himself or had sought privacy when he needed a release, but now he was happy to let his boys pleasure him in plain sight. It was almost a daily occurrence to find Brad on his knees at some point, and it was a toss-up as to whether he'd be naked or not.

"You're a halfway decent dancer, Flint," Connor said.

"You were worried about your toes?"

"It's not like you're known for being graceful," Connor replied, and Noah loved that he dared to make that joke, considering Noah's leg and everything.

"Unlike those two," Noah said, and Connor turned them around so they could watch Indy and Josh, who had eyes for nothing but each other, swaying to their own rhythm.

Noah let out a soft sigh, his heart filling with love all over again. "We did good, Connor."

Connor's grip on him tightened for a moment. "Thanks for leading that particular way," he mumbled. "I was so scared of losing Josh, but you showed me I had nothing to fear."

Noah leaned back so he could see the man's eyes. "I don't think it's possible for someone to love you more than Josh does. What he and Indy have, it has nothing to do with us. It's like that love exists on a different plane, you know?"

Connor nodded. "Yeah, I know that now. Took me a while to get there though, and I needed you to show me the way. So thank you."

Noah smiled. "You getting mushy on me, O'Connor?"

He was expecting Connor to say something snarky back, as they'd been doing since they met, but instead, the man stopped dancing. He let go of Noah's hand, then grabbed his face with both hands and planted a firm kiss on his mouth.

"You need to learn how to take a damn compliment, Flint."

4

J osh gasped as he caught the kiss from the corner of
his eye.

"Connor just kissed Noah," he whispered in
Indy's ear, turning them both so they could watch.

"You're kidding me," Indy said, disbelief dripping from
his voice.

Josh couldn't blame him. Though they had been tolerant
with each other and had grown close, there had never been
more between Noah and Connor. Sure, they had no
problem being naked around each other, and they sure as
hell liked to watch the other fuck, but that was as far as it
went. They joked about it sometimes, Josh and Indy, what it
would take to get those two to do more. Because there *was*
something there, that alpha rivalry sizzling just a little
hotter than mere friendship.

Josh turned his attention back to Indy when Noah and
Connor resumed dancing—though the fact they were doing
that was a miracle all on its own. "How are you feeling,
baby?" he asked Indy, who had nestled his head again
against Josh's shoulder.

"Perfect. Like I'm in heaven. Best day ever."

Josh hummed in contentment, as he felt the same way. He put his head on Indy's, resting his cheek against those soft curls. Noah and Connor were still dancing, their bodies closer than Josh would've expected. Many of the guests watched them with big smiles on their faces, though Miles and Brad were sneaking out, Josh noticed, probably for a quick release since it had been a few hours for Miles.

Aaron had slid off his chair and was sitting at Blake's feet, Blake's hand scratching his neck. Josh expected his brother to start licking Blake any second now. It was adorable, the way Aaron surrendered to Blake. Josh had caught him once in full puppy mode when he'd dropped by unannounced to drop off some clothes and supplies for Blake's closet. The man still offered a safe place for victims of domestic abuse, and Josh was all too happy to contribute.

Aaron had been wearing a puppy mask...and nothing else. Well, unless you counted the butt plug with the cute tail he'd been sporting. Or the collar and leash, which had been pink with rhinestones. Josh had merely blinked, even if it had been a bit more than he'd expected to see of his younger brother. It was easy to see how much it meant to Aaron and Blake, so who was he to judge?

Besides, Josh himself had been standing there with his cock cage on and a fiery red ass under his jeans, still smarting something fierce from the paddling Connor had administrated the day before. Kinky fuckers, that's what they were. All of them. And Josh couldn't care less, could only be happy that he'd found his real family, his tribe.

The song ended and the next one started, an equally slow number. With the kind of people they'd invited to the wedding, they'd figured real dancing wasn't gonna happen anyway, so they'd chosen slow songs perfect for romance and maybe a little making out.

As if reading his mind, Indy pulled his head low and pressed their lips together. Josh opened up for him, like he always did. He couldn't explain how, but Indy had the key to his heart like no one else. Connor was his strong man, his fire, the fierce want that thundered through his veins every time Josh looked at him. But Indy? Indy was his center, his compass.

And so he kissed him, slowly and thoroughly, their tongues engaging in an age-old dance, their bodies pressed as close together as possible. All time ceased to exist, their surroundings fading away as they danced and kissed.

After two songs, Connor stepped in to dance with Josh while Indy switched to Noah.

"I apologize in advance," Connor said with a hint of embarrassment. "You know I can't dance for shit."

"Like I care," Josh said, wrapping his arms around him and pulling him so close a sheet of paper wouldn't have fit between their bodies. "All I want for you to do is hold me."

"I can do that," Connor said, then put his cheek against Josh's.

It was moments like this that Josh was reminded he was taller than Connor by an inch or so. He rarely felt it, because Connor's build more than made up for it, but now he noticed it. Wasn't it funny that even though he was taller, he felt smaller? It was fine with him. He'd long accepted his submissive nature, which was such a perfect match with Connor's dominant side.

Connor's hands lowered to his ass, and he pulled Josh even closer, bringing their hard cocks in close contact. "I can't wait for tonight," Josh whispered. "Fuck, I missed you."

It was his own fault, for insisting they'd spend the day

before the wedding apart. Boy, had he regretted that decision.

"I missed you, too, baby. Let's never do that again."

"Mmm," Josh agreed.

"Was this day how you had dreamed it would be?" Connor asked.

Josh leaned back to check his expression, concerned for a second Connor was worried about something, but he saw nothing but love. He put his cheek back against Connor's with a happy sigh.

"It was. I loved how relaxed it was, not so formal and stuffy."

"That wouldn't have fit us at all."

"And baby," he leaned back again, because he wanted to look Connor in the eyes when he said this. "Thank you for allowing Indy and me the first dance. That meant the world to us."

Connor's face broke open in a soft smile. "You're welcome, baby. I love watching the two of you."

Josh giggled. "You love watching in general," he dared to joke.

Connor chuckled with him. "You know me so well. Thank you for accepting me the way I am," he then said, sobering.

"Oh god, baby, that's right back atcha. I love we can be ourselves with each other, and with the crazy friends we've surrounded ourselves with."

"We're lucky," Connor said.

Josh nodded, then put his head back against Connor's. "Yeah."

It must have been maybe an hour later, after Josh had made out with Connor and Indy and had danced till the point where his feet started hurting, when Aaron came up to him. "We're leaving," he announced.

"You don't have to," Josh protested, but Aaron smiled.

"You guys need your privacy, and I'm too grateful for our relationship now to risk it by overstaying my welcome."

He had a point, Josh had to admit. Out of consideration for Aaron and Blake, who were kinky in their own way but weren't fans of either watching or engaging in public sex, they always toned things down when those two were present. Miles did the same, seeking more privacy when Aaron and Blake were around, as not to frustrate them. And Josh had to admit that things were heating up, though they'd kept themselves in check seeing as there were still guests present.

"You're probably right," Josh admitted with a smile.

Aaron reached out for a hug, and Josh's heart warmed. They'd come far, he and his brother, melting the ice between them bit by bit. Being with Blake had done wonders for Aaron's self-confidence, and Josh had come to see how troubled his brother had been. He hugged him tight, then kissed his head.

"Thank you," Josh said. "It means so much to me you were here today."

"I wouldn't have missed it for the world. Now, go be with your men. I'm so, so happy for you," Aaron said, his voice a little choked up.

Josh leaned back to study his face. It showed happiness, but there was more. "What's wrong?" he asked.

Aaron shook his head. "Nothing. Nothing important," he added when Josh sent him a look of disbelief.

"Aaron," Josh said, his voice filling with concern. "Talk to me. What is it?"

Aaron glanced over his shoulder at Blake, who was

engaged in a conversation with Noah and Indy. He turned back to Josh and bit his lip. "I should be grateful, you know?" he whispered. "When I met him, Blake didn't even want a commitment, and now he's with me. And we're happy together, we are. He takes such good care of me."

Understanding filled Josh. "You're ready for more."

Aaron nodded. "Watching you guys today...it's what I've always wanted. I've always wanted to be married, to belong with someone, even though I didn't understand why I struggled picturing myself as the one taking care of someone else in that scenario. Now, with Blake, it's all I want, for him to take care of me, to be my..."

He stopped talking, his eyes filling with insecurity, but Josh understood. "You want Blake to be your owner and make it official. I get it."

Aaron's eyes teared up. "It's crazy, right? It's too fast, too much. I'm setting myself up for a major disappointment here."

Josh cupped his brother's cheeks. "The heart wants what it wants. That's never wrong." He kissed his forehead, then let go. "Look at me and Indy. By all accounts, I should've been happy with Connor, and I was, but my heart still yearned for Indy. You can't help who you love, Aaron, and you shouldn't apologize for what you want."

"Not even if I'll get my heart broken?" Aaron whispered.

Josh smiled. "I think you underestimate Blake's love for you. There's nothing that man wouldn't do for you."

"I don't want him to ask me because he feels like he should or because it's what I want," Aaron protested. "I want him to ask me because it's what he wants."

"Look, it may not come natural to him considering his background, okay? Getting married is a big step for him, much more than for any of us." Aaron had shared enough of

Blake's story for Josh to understand the man had some serious trauma when it came to relationships. "But he loves you. Hell, he's devoted to you. If you show him this is what you want, he'll meet you halfway, like he always has."

Aaron's eyes lit up. "I know he loves me. He shows me every day."

"Then trust in that, and don't worry about everything else. He won't break your heart, at least not intentionally. You may have to give him a little nudge, though, since he may not realize this is what you want."

Aaron looked pensive, but then he smiled. "You're right. Thank you."

Josh smiled back as he hugged him again. "You're welcome. Thanks so much for celebrating with us today."

"Anytime. Now, go have sex," Aaron joked.

Josh caught the heated look in Connor's eyes as he watched him, and he swallowed, his cock already growing hard. "Yeah, that sounds like a plan. A very, very good plan."

BY NATURE, Connor was a patient man, but he was seconds away from kicking Aaron and Blake out. All the other guests were filing out, leaving just the four of them and Miles and his boys. The latter, Connor considered family.

Well, Blake and Aaron were family too, even more since Aaron was actually related by blood, but it was different. He liked them, had come to appreciate Aaron more and more, and he'd never forget Blake's role in fighting off the attackers who'd come to their house. The man had saved their lives, no doubt about it. But they were not the kind of family you could do anything you wanted around, unlike Miles, Brad, and Charlie, who didn't blink an eye when they saw Connor naked. Or worse.

And right now, Connor wanted to get naked. Badly. Not just that, but he wanted to strip Josh out of that sexy, form-fitting suit he was wearing, bend him over whatever table was closest, and sink himself inside that tight heat. He hadn't fucked him in two days—Josh insisting it would make their wedding night more special. In Connor's opinion, fucking Josh was always special, no matter how often he did it, but he'd been overruled. So he'd sucked it up and had waited, but now his patience was wearing thin.

He'd been eying Josh's ass all day, perfectly outlined in that suit, beckoning him like a damn beacon. At first, the wedding itself had taken precedence, but his cock now insisted it was time to move on to more carnal pleasures. The Beast could only be denied for so long—and yes, Connor had finally caved in and called his dick by the same nickname everyone used. There was only so long he'd been able to hold out when it was a compliment, really, and it was said with an awe that made him feel proud about his cock.

Just then, Josh looked over his shoulder and smiled. He gave Aaron a last hug, and then the little pup made his way over to Blake, who was finishing up his goodbyes with Noah and Josh. Blake smiled as he pulled Aaron close, and then they walked out.

"Inside," Connor growled, closing the distance between him and Josh in a few long strides.

Josh pouted in that cute way that made Connor want to kiss him breathless. "But Connor, I wanted to dance some more..."

Connor grabbed his tie, then pulled him close until their faces were less than an inch apart. "Don't you worry, baby, I'll make you dance. All fucking night long."

He kissed him hard, his hand finding that perfect ass and squeezing it. "Now, get your lovely ass inside, strip the fuck out of that suit so I don't have to ruin it, and wait for me there."

Josh's eyes darkened. "Yes, Connor."

He rushed inside, a giggling Indy on his heels.

"You guys go inside," Miles said, dragging his eyes away from Brad and Charlie, who were slow dancing, kissing each other with abandon. "I'll turn off everything here before we head inside the house as well."

Connor watched Brad and Charlie. He'd wondered at times how it could work, those three men, since they were so different. Miles was as steady as they came, the anchor that kept them in place. He loved his boys so much, and it showed in every little thing he did. Charlie was their joy, blossoming into his full, extravagant self now that he'd overcome his trauma. And Brad, Brad was the glue, his need for them so big and so deep that Connor wondered if it would ever go away. Yet every time he needed, Miles and Charlie supplied, and that raw edge that had always characterized Brad was fading, morphing into a sweet contentment.

"I can't get over how much he's changing," Connor said.

Miles followed his eyes. "Brad?"

Connor nodded. "Yeah. It's amazing to see."

Miles let out a happy hum of agreement. "You all play a crucial part in that as well. It's not just me and Charlie."

A few weeks ago, Miles had needed to leave for a few days for work training. Connor had taken over the daily morning spanking for Brad and had made sure the boy got attention throughout those days. Brad's quiet approval had shown how much he had appreciated it.

"I know," Connor said. "He makes it easy because you can tell how much he needs it."

Miles turned toward him, his eyes careful as he spoke. "This may be the worst timing in the world, considering it's your wedding day, but I just wanted to say it. You have our permission to use Brad, if Josh would be okay with it."

Connor frowned. What was Miles talking about? "Use him?"

"Yeah. Have him blow you...or fuck him."

Connor's eyes widened. "You're shitting me."

"It shouldn't be a secret to you he's a little slut. He loves being used, and it's not exclusive to us. If you or Noah need or want him, he'd love to oblige—but only if Indy and Josh are on board with it. He'd never come between you, you know that."

Connor's head dazzled. This was a somewhat unexpected development, and yet it felt natural, as if everything they'd done so far had come to this. But he couldn't accept this, right? He had Josh. And Noah had Indy. Brad didn't fit into that picture...did he?

Miles's hand came down on his shoulder. "As I said, worst timing in the world. Think about it or don't, it's up to you, but I wanted you to know."

There was nothing but sincerity in the man's voice, and Connor let out a sigh. "Thank you, I guess. I'm gonna need some time to mull this over."

With a last squeeze, Miles let go of his shoulder. "No rush. The offer has no expiration date. And I know you never rush into anything."

The man knew him well enough, Connor thought. "True."

"Go inside. Your man is waiting for you," Miles said with a laugh, and Connor realized Noah was also waiting for him, shooting him a look that was none too patient.

"Hold your horses, Flint, I'm coming," he called out.

"No, you're not, and that's the whole problem. Get a fucking move on, O'Connor. I wanna get a start on the wedding night."

Connor grinned, couldn't help it. He shot Miles a laugh and made his way to Noah. He hadn't planned on it, but the words rolled off his tongue. "Miles just offered we can use Brad if we want, have him suck us off or even fuck him."

Noah's mouth pulled up in a wicked grin. "He's such a little slut. He's been dying for your cock since the first time he got his eyes on it."

"The invitation was for us both."

"Sure." Noah grinned. "But I'm more of an afterthought. With me, he's offering because he thinks it'll make me happy. With you, it's selfish. He craves the Beast, man."

"He does?" Connor mentally shook his head. How the fuck was it possible that Noah had seen this, that he wasn't even surprised in the least?

"Connor," Noah said, his voice much warmer now and devoid of the teasing. "I know this is harder for you than it is for me or for some of us. You're a man who thinks in clear patterns, who needs rules."

"You mean I'm boring and old-fashioned," Connor said, not able to quite keep the bitterness out of his voice. He'd been the one with the most resistance to Josh and Indy, he knew that all too well. It had taken him time to understand that Josh could love him and Indy both, that it wasn't one or the other.

"No," Noah said with force. "It's how you're wired. Look, me and Josh had a fucked-up thing from the beginning. It's made it easier for us to accept that things aren't always black and white."

"You'd better not refer to me and a certain number of

shades of gray in one sentence," Connor threatened him, but his frustration with himself retreated.

Noah grinned. "I'm not quite that stupid." Then his face sobered. "I've never fit into any box, so I'm a little less bound by what's considered 'normal' than you are. There's nothing wrong with that, but neither is there anything wrong with you. I know things like this are new to you and that you need time to consider it. So take your time."

"Miles said the offer didn't have an expiration date," Connor admitted.

"There you go. He knows damn well you wouldn't jump on this right away."

"It feels wrong to even consider it. Like it's..." He didn't dare say the word, especially not on his wedding day.

"It's not cheating, Connor. Not with Brad. Not if Josh knows and is fine with it. Not if we do it all in the open."

Connor tried to picture it, Brad's tight body taking the Beast. The thought made him even harder. "I'll think about it," he conceded. "But not right now."

"Hell no. Right now, we enjoy the best part of getting married," Noah said. "A fuckfest that lasts all night."

5

He was *married*. Josh let that thought sink in as he kneeled next to the bed, naked. He was married to Connor now, taking his name.

Joshua O'Connor.

The rush rolled through him all over again. He truly belonged to him now in every aspect. Who would've ever thought this was where their road would lead to when they'd met during that robbery that seemed like a lifetime ago? Theirs hadn't been an easy journey, especially when they'd had to pretend to break up to save Indy. Those had been dark weeks that Josh had survived only by sheer determination and the knowledge it would be worth it.

And it had been. The day Indy had come home, Josh had known he'd do it all over again to ensure his freedom. No one had ever linked him or Connor to the shooting in Boston, though the FBI had sure tried. But Josh's breakdown at the psychiatric facility had been well-documented, his doctors assuring the FBI Josh had been drugged within an inch of his sanity.

And Connor, why, he'd been working undercover for the

Boston PD all that time, hadn't he? At least, that's what he kept telling the FBI, and he'd been backed up by the Boston cops all the way. Josh still wasn't sure how Connor had pulled that part off, but he had. The FBI had stopped actively investigating the shooting for now with the promise to the public to reopen it should new evidence become available.

Of course, the investigation into the Fitzpatricks was steaming ahead at full speed. Indy had already spent a few days talking to the new DA, and the case was expected to go to trial in a few weeks. Not before Christmas, the DA had promised, so Indy could at least spend that time at home. After that, it was a big unknown how long the trial would last and how long Indy's testimony would take. He was the star witness, that much had become clear.

Indy had flat out refused to relocate to a safe house, even though Noah, Connor, and Josh had indicated they'd come with him. He'd told them he was done running and that he would stand his ground. Josh understood, even if it scared the fuck out of him. Yes, Duncan Fitzpatrick was dead, and so were the other top leaders of their organization, but Josh wasn't stupid enough to think it would crumble, not even after the endless raids the Boston PD had done.

"Baby, you're frowning," Indy's soft voice interrupted his thoughts.

Josh looked up to find him on the bed on his stomach, his hands under his chin as he studied Josh. Indy reached out and caressed the worry line between Josh's eyebrows.

"What's got you worried?"

Josh hesitated. His wedding night was not the right time for this. It would ruin the mood.

"Oh baby, don't shut me out," Indy pleaded.

"It's not the conversation we should be having today of

all days," Josh said. He broke posture and grabbed Indy's hand, kissing it before lacing his fingers through it. "It would spoil the mood."

Indy pursed his lips. "If it's worrying you right now, it's important enough to talk about right now."

Josh turned sideways so his face was at the same level as Indy's and let his head rest on Indy's shoulder, his nose buried in his neck. He breathed him in deeply, the smell alone enough to make him calmer. "You're so sweet."

Indy's hand found his hair, and he caressed him, as usual content to wait till Josh was ready to talk. He still debated if he should, even though he knew he couldn't keep this from Indy. Or from Connor and Noah. They all read him like a book, and though his PTSD had been stable, he still struggled with flare-ups. All three of them knew how to ground him, and even Miles had intervened a few weeks ago when a car backfiring had startled him too much.

It used to bother him, this dependence on others, this weakness, but that had changed. Instead, he'd grown thankful for the family he had around him, for the men in his life dedicated to taking care of him. He'd stopped resisting it and instead embraced the love behind it. It was that same love that made him realize he should talk to Indy.

"I'm worried about you, about the trial," he whispered, his face still pressed against Indy.

Indy's hand tightened for a second or two before he relaxed again. "You're scared someone will still come after me?"

"You're the key witness, baby," Josh said. "Without you, they'd have a hell of a time getting convictions."

Indy gently grabbed his neck, then pulled him back so their eyes met. "I'm sorry, I didn't consider not going into a safe house would cause you stress," he said.

Josh let out a sigh, already feeling better now he'd shared his worries. "To be fair, staying in a safe house would've freaked me the fuck out as well."

"It's hard to do what we do, to live how we live, when we're under constant surveillance," Indy agreed. "That's why I wanted to stay here, in our own home, where we at least have the freedom to do what we want. I didn't think you'd do well without your sessions with Connor."

Josh considered that. "True. And we'd miss Miles and the boys something fierce."

Indy smiled. "There's something strangely comforting about watching Brad on his knees, isn't there?"

There sure was, but not as much comfort in simply having his family around him. Josh wasn't sure when it had happened, but somewhere in the last few months, he'd become that person who wasn't happy until everyone was home. Boring, maybe, but he didn't care.

"We should consider hiring extra protection," Connor spoke up from the doorway. Josh hadn't even noticed him and Noah standing there. "I agree with Indy that a safe house would be too disruptive, not only for you, baby, but for all of us. But if it makes you feel safer, we can look into hiring private protection."

"They'd have to be gay-friendly and kink-proof," Noah said, and Josh realized he was only half-joking. "I don't want people around us who judge us for how we live. Ain't nobody got time for that."

"Good point," Connor said, nodding. "Would that work for you, Indy?"

Indy gave Josh a long look, then nodded when he was apparently satisfied with what he saw. "It seems like a reasonable compromise. Plus, the DA said once the trial starts, it's not only threats we have to worry about. The press may be an issue as well. We don't want reporters swarming our property either."

"I'll look into it. Miles may have connections," Connor promised. He walked over to Josh and put his strong hand on Josh's neck. "Does that settle your stress, baby?"

Josh nodded, then looked up to Connor. "I'm sorry I didn't tell you."

Connor bent over to kiss his lips, a soft, sweet kiss. "You told Indy. That's good enough, baby. As long as you talk to someone and don't keep it in, it's all good." A laugh sparkled in his eyes. "Unless you want me to punish you for this, in which case I'd be more than happy to oblige."

Josh's look was pure adoration. The man knew him so well. "Yes, please, Connor."

Connor pulled him to his feet effortlessly, slapping his ass with a sharp sting. "My pleasure, baby."

Josh reached for his belt, but Connor stopped him. "Before we get to that, Noah and I had a little something for the two of you."

He shared a look with Noah and they both took out a little velvet box from their pockets. What was that? The boxes were flicked open and Connor presented his to Josh, while Noah did the same with Indy. Josh gasped when he spotted the gorgeous ring.

"We didn't want to give these in front of everyone, because they're engraved in a special way," Noah said.

Connor took out the ring and showed it to Josh. It was a simple design, four little diamonds on a white gold ring. Josh teared up when he realized what the four diamonds symbolized.

"We know there's four of us in this relationship, in this marriage, and Noah and I felt the rings should symbolize that," Connor said, his voice raw with emotions. "Look inside."

He gave Josh the ring and he turned it to look at the inscription. Noah - Indy - Josh - Connor, it read. All four names. Not two, not three, but all four of them.

"Baby," Josh said, unable to form the words to express how he felt. It was so big, this feeling of belonging, of home, of finding the love he never believed could be real. "That's so beautiful."

He gave it back to Connor and extended his hand so Connor could put it on. It took a little wriggling, but then it slid on, and Josh's eyes teared up even more.

"It looks perfect on the two of you," Noah said with the same choked-up voice they all had.

Josh let himself fall against Connor, wrapping his arms tight around him. "I love you, so much. That's so perfect."

"Good. I'm so glad you love it."

He held him for a few seconds more, then gently slapped him on his ass. "I think there's something else you're gonna love."

It was the worst segue in history, but Josh didn't care. He loved knowing how much his man wanted him. "Yes, Connor."

Connor slapped him again before his fingers found the little flared end of Josh's plug. He grabbed hold of it, wiggled it a little, but enough to make Josh moan. "What's this, baby? You prepped for me?"

Josh's "Yes, Connor" was more of a breath of anticipation.

"You in a hurry, baby?" Connor wiggled the plug again.

"I need you inside me. It's been two days..." Josh heard the little whine in his own voice.

"May I remind you who came up with that stupid plan?"

Josh sent him a sweet smile. "Imagine how much better it'll feel now to fuck me hard?" he said, his voice hopeful.

"Oh baby, it always feels good, no matter how long or short it has been. You always take my breath away."

Josh melted against Connor, even as the man took his mouth in a deep, wet kiss.

"Damn, that was pure poetry," Noah mumbled.

"He just raised the bar for you," Indy commented, and even through the daze of Connor's kiss, Josh heard the laughter in his voice.

"He raised something else as well," Noah replied, laughing, and then Josh stopped listening because Connor overwhelmed his senses, as usual.

Josh's hands found Connor's belt all by themselves, and seconds later, he'd unzipped him and pulled his pants down. Just before he could curl his hand around the Beast, Connor grabbed his wrist. He broke off the kiss and sent Josh a heated look.

"I'm gonna use your ass as a little cum dumpster tonight, baby. And you're not gonna spill a drop, you hear me? I'm gonna plug you in between and then fill you up all over again until you're one big, sloppy mess."

Josh's heart started singing. "Yes, Connor."

"And you don't get to come until I'm spent."

"Yes, Connor."

"Glad we understand each other. Now, bend over that damn bed and spread your legs. Enough talking."

Josh was already moving. "Yes, Connor."

Within seconds, Connor had lubed the Beast. With one firm pull, he removed the plug from Josh's ass and lined up, not even waiting for Josh to get ready but plunging in. It was a good thing the plug he'd been wearing had been big, but even now, Connor's dick breached him until tears formed in his eyes. The best kind of tears, the kind that made his head go blank with contentment.

Connor kept pushing until he bottomed out, Josh letting out groans as he tried to adjust. Connor's hand pushed him into the mattress, his massive cock spearing him like he was prey.

"Joshua O'Connor, there is no sweeter place on this entire planet than right here, buried inside you."

"There he goes with the poetry again. Marriage is making him mushy already," Noah commented.

"Fuck off, Flint. You're just jealous and feeling inadequate."

Josh laughed, his laughter transforming into a low, deep moan when Connor pulled back and rammed in again.

"Yes, Connor. Please, Connor, more."

6

————

The sight of that monster cock disappearing into Josh never failed to arouse Noah. Not that he'd needed much arousing. He'd been pretty much hard the entire day out of sheer excitement. Indy was his, wearing his ring, carrying his name. Still, he didn't turn down a good view of Connor taking Josh—and neither did Indy, who made room for Noah on the bed so they could watch together.

Noah stripped out of his suit, even remembering to drape it over a chair rather than leave it crumpled on the floor. That should make Charlie happy. And Josh, who was in charge of all laundry. He also took his prosthesis off, dumping that on the floor unceremoniously. His leg was doing much better after the second amputation, and he was at a point where he felt comfortable and self-confident enough.

"They're so beautiful," Indy said dreamily. "Sometimes it's hard to believe how happy we are."

"You deserve all the happiness in the world," Noah said

as he lowered himself on the bed next to him, his voice cracking.

Indy's eyes shifted from the live porn in front of them to Noah. "And you were dissing Connor for getting mushy."

"I know, I know. It's just..." He sighed. "You feel it even more on a day like this."

Indy snuggled close, his slim body seeking Noah's embrace. "I said the same thing to Miles this morning, like how I'm almost feeling guilty for being this happy."

Noah had no trouble imagining that. "It's been one hell of a year. Not having to look over your shoulder and being able to relax is gonna take some getting used to."

"I'm not there yet," Indy admitted. "And I don't think I will be until the trial is behind us."

Noah kissed him softly, the two of them in a world of their own, even as the bed shook with the force of Connor fucking Josh. "I like Connor's proposal of hiring private security."

"Can we afford that? I'm sure that's not cheap."

Noah had been appointed the financial guy for the whole house, with assistance from Brad, who was way better at the math of it and putting numbers into impressive spread sheets but less talented in the practical aspects of translating those numbers into goals and plans for the future. With three full-time salaries—Miles, Connor, and Brad—and a little extra income from Charlie, they were doing well, even with Noah still working on his degree, Josh contributing with the few hours he made as a shooting instructor, and Indy only picking up the occasional payments for jiu jitsu classes.

"We'll make it work. Leave the details to me and Connor."

Indy grinned. "Is that code for 'Don't worry your pretty little head over it?'"

"I'm much, much smarter than that."

"Yes, you are. Thank you for taking such good care of me, of us."

"It's my pleasure," Noah said, and he meant it.

Indy's soft hand stroked his back, and Noah wanted to purr like a kitten. He leaned into the touch, closing his eyes.

"You're so beautiful," Indy said in that dreamy tone that never failed to hit Noah deep.

That was love, he supposed. That you could look at another person and not see their faults and shortcomings, not see their scars and imperfections, but to see beauty.

"You still think so?" he asked, opening his eyes again to find Indy studying him.

"That first time I met you, I thought you were hot but stern. Aloof. And then you smiled at me for the first time, and you made my heart stumble. You still do that to me, Noah. Every time you smile at me, I fall in love with you all over again."

How much love could a heart hold? His felt like his was bursting, and he leaned in for a kiss, Indy willingly opening for him. It was slow, sweet, the kiss of lovers who knew each other well. Their heat burned slow tonight, an unhurried flame content to take its time.

They both rolled on their sides, Indy sneaking a leg between Noah's, with him putting his leg around Indy's body. He loved how it felt, that small body against his, that strength that radiated from Indy's every move.

"I only have to see you walk into a room and my heart trips over itself," Noah whispered against his lips.

Indy smiled. "You going poetic on me, baby?"

Noah cupped his cheeks. "I'd write love songs for you if I could."

Indy's eyes went soft and dreamy again. "I don't need those. The way you look at me, the way you treat me, it says it all." He kissed Noah, a mere brush of his lips. "Make love to me, baby. Show me with your body how much you love me."

Noah caught Indy's bottom lip between his teeth in a gentle bite. "With pleasure."

He nibbled along his lip, greedily taking in the little gasps Indy made into his mouth, then soothed with his tongue. The bed was still shaking with the force of Connor, who was going to town on Josh's ass, forbidding him to come, of course. But Noah was in his own world, only seeing Indy. His cheeks were rosy, his eyes glazed, and his lips all swollen from Noah's kisses.

Noah pushed against him lightly, still careful not to use any force with Indy. When Indy rolled on his back, Noah covered his body with his own, then started a slow descent with his mouth. He pressed kisses along Indy's jaw, moving down his neck to his collarbones. His right hand found Indy's nipples, which he rolled and pressed until they became hard pebbles.

God, his skin was so smooth here, so soft. His mouth followed his fingers, sucking those pebbles until Indy was squirming underneath him, bucking his hips in search of friction.

"Noah!" he cried out in a mix of demanding and begging.

Noah never could deny him. He didn't have Connor's streak of Dom-meanness, where he could deny Josh for hours. Noah always gave in because he wanted nothing more than to pleasure Indy. So his hand traveled lower and wrapped around Indy's leaking cock, so perfect in his hand. He was still insecure at times about his size, but Noah had worshiped his body enough now that Indy knew it didn't matter to him.

He licked a trail from his bellybutton down, replacing his hand with his mouth. Indy's cock felt so perfect in his mouth, and Noah loved swallowing him deep. He pressed his tongue against the underside, increasing the sucking pressure, and the moan that Indy let out was music to his ears.

He released his dick for a moment to lavish his balls with attention. There was a spot that Indy loved... He found it, right behind his balls, and Indy bucked against him.

"Noah!" he moaned again, and to Noah, that was more beautiful than any love song.

Noah folded his legs back, as always thanking his lucky stars for how flexible Indy was, which opened him wide for Noah's erotic exploration. The scars on his back extended to one of his ass cheeks, and Noah never failed to kiss it. He loved every single one of them. Others might call them disfiguring, but to Noah they were a testament to Indy's strength and character.

He traced that big, thick scar with his tongue, then allowed himself to continue the path and tongue his crack. He wasn't much for teasing, as he lacked the patience to draw it out, but he loved driving Indy crazy with want, and he was well on his way now. One lap over his hole, and then he dug in, tonguing Indy's ass as he exploded in an intoxicating soundtrack of pants and moans and little squeals, all of them cheering Noah on.

"Oh god, Noah, you have to... I can't take it anymore. Please, Noah, please!"

Noah smiled against his fluttering hole, so pretty and

pink, so welcoming. He wet his fingers and slid one in, curling it to find that famous spot where Indy was so freaking sensitive. It was easy to find by now, familiar as he was with his body, but as usual, Indy reacted as if he'd been shocked.

"Oh there, baby, right there. That feels so good."

He pressed in a second finger, then wrapped his mouth around Indy's cock. It wouldn't take long now, and he wanted to taste him. Indy's body shuddered and shook, and then he surrendered himself to his orgasm. His cock twitched and his body convulsed around Noah's fingers as he came in his mouth, Noah hungrily swallowing every last drop.

Noah rested against Indy's ass, panting himself a little from the effort. His cock was leaking and his balls full, but his heart was even fuller. God, he was perfect, his Indy.

CONNOR HELD JOSH, who lay splayed across his body, the evidence of the massive orgasm he'd had between them. Next to them, Noah and Indy were lazily making out after a round of lovemaking that had made Connor feel all mushy.

"How are you feeling, baby?" Connor asked.

"Ungh."

Connor smiled. "You still with me?"

"Mfrgh."

Connor loved it when he wore Josh out to the point where he was barely able to form coherent words anymore, let alone sentences. He stroked his back with long, calming touches. Josh rubbed his cheek against Connor's chest, then let out another content sigh.

With a smile on his face, Connor roamed Josh's back

with his hands, then trailed lower to his ass. As if on cue, Josh spread his legs a little. He knew Connor so well. It wasn't that he had any plans to fuck him again. Josh was worn out after three strenuous rounds—and yes, Connor had plugged him in between—and besides, Connor himself was blissed out.

No, he loved to feel it, and his right hand found it with ease. His cum trickling out of Josh's hole. Three loads of it, to be precise. Connor had no idea why it made him feel the way it did, but he couldn't deny it sent a rush through him, this irrefutable evidence he'd claimed him. Apparently, there was still a caveman deep inside him who wanted to show who Josh belonged to.

When he'd satisfied himself with that check, he kissed Josh's head, and rolled over to deposit him on his back. "I'm gonna clean you up, baby. You stay here."

Josh's answer was another unintelligible mumble, which Connor took as consent. He rolled off the bed and walked into the bathroom, where he first relieved himself and then washed his chest and groin with a washcloth. He rinsed it out and headed back into the bedroom, where he found Josh now curled up against Indy's back, who let out a soft giggle.

"You're sticky, baby. Let Connor clean you first."

"Mmm. Wanna hold you," Josh mumbled, half asleep by the looks of it.

Even a few months ago, this would've made Connor insecure, his man seeking Indy for comfort rather than him, but now, all he felt was love. How could you not when you watched those two?

Indy looked at him over Josh's shoulder. "Give me the cloth. I'll clean him."

Connor climbed back in bed and handed Indy the cloth.

Josh protested as he was rolled on his back and Indy cleaned him, then threw the cloth with a nice aim straight onto the bathroom floor.

Josh rolled right back on his side and curled up against Indy. He was asleep before Indy had put his head against his shoulder.

"He's worn out," Indy said, almost apologetic, though he sounded sleepy himself.

"It's fine. It was a lot for him, a full program like today, with all the stress he had over messing it up with an episode," Connor said.

He hugged Josh from behind, finding a spot for his arm where he didn't bother Indy. They'd learned to share Josh in bed, just like Noah now spooned Indy from the back, accommodating his need to be close to Josh as well. Indy's eyes fluttered close, Connor saw, and seconds later, he was asleep.

"He did well today," Noah said softly.

"He did," Connor replied, feeling proud.

Josh had come far in the last few months. His PTSD was stable, with a flare-up now and then, but manageable. And he excelled in his part-time job as a shooting instructor, the Albany PD singing his praises at every turn.

"You're good for him, Connor. You truly bring out the best of him."

Connor blinked. "Thank you," he said, letting the magnitude of that moment sink in, then realized it was only half of the truth. "We're good for him, the four of us. It's not me or Indy or you. It's us together."

Both their eyes were drawn to the sleeping men between them, and Noah's face softened in the same way that Connor felt himself react.

"We're good for all of us," Noah said.

"Who woulda thought when I responded to that robbery?" Connor said, almost laughing when he remembered it. "I could barely recall my own name after seeing Josh. It was like being struck by lightning."

Noah chuckled. "I loved how you came to our house to see him again, making up some lame-ass excuse."

Connor rubbed his chin. "That wasn't very subtle, was it? I had no idea what I was doing. All I knew was that I needed to see him again."

"It's not like I can make fun of you, seeing how I fell for Indy from the second I met him."

"He's special," Connor agreed. "He and Josh are two of the strongest people I've ever met."

Noah cocked his head, meeting his eyes over the two sleeping bodies between them. "You're not so bad yourself, Connor."

"You starting to like me, Flint?" Connor joked, his insides warm with Noah's compliment.

"Well, you kissed me, so I kinda feel obligated, you know?"

They both smiled, an easy camaraderie between them that Connor would've never thought possible a year ago. "If you call that a kiss, we need to talk. That was a mere peck."

Then Noah's hand reached over Indy and Josh to find Connor's, covering it with his own and squeezing it. "All jokes aside, Connor. I hope you realize that you've become my best friend. I'm so grateful you're in my life."

Connor's mouth dropped open. That was not what he'd been expecting at all. "But...but what about Josh? And Miles?"

Noah smiled at him, not letting go of his hand. "You know how complicated my relationship with Josh has always been. There's so much history there, that it's a struggle sometimes to allow myself to change in my interaction with him rather than fall back on how we've always been, if that makes sense. And Miles, it's different. I love the guy to pieces, and I couldn't be happier he's living with us, but it's not the same. You challenge me, and you inspire me to be a better man, and you're there when I need you. You're my best friend, Connor. Just accept it."

Connor's head was scrambling, trying to come up with something, anything. But all he had was a bone-deep gratitude. He didn't have Noah's words or his psychological insights. Hell, until Noah had just spoken, Connor hadn't even realized he felt the same way about him. When the fuck had that happened? When had he stopped tolerating Noah and had started...loving him? It was the weirdest thing, to be confronted with your own emotions like that.

"I'm...I'm speechless. I legit don't know what to say."

Noah grinned as he let go of Connor's hand, but it was a kind grin, one that said he understood. "Tell me you love me too, so we can get some sleep."

That quip restarted Connor's brain. "What happened to the all-night fuckfest you promised?"

Noah shot a poignant look at Indy and Josh. "These two are out for the count, so unless you wanted to get to second base with me, sleep it is."

Connor was still smiling when he closed his eyes and settled in for the night, but the last thought he had before falling asleep was of him kissing Noah again. Weird.

7

There were few things Charlie took more seriously than decorating a Christmas tree. Makeup, maybe. Or shoes. But this time of year, getting the tree just right was crucial to the holiday spirit, Charlie felt.

At first, he'd been a tad concerned with the lack of enthusiasm for this project from the others. Brad had given him a blank look, as if he wasn't even sure what a Christmas tree was. Heathen. Miles hadn't been jumping for joy either, but Charlie would turn him around. He was sure of it.

The good news about no one else giving a flying fuck was that he had free rein. He'd asked Miles for a budget, and Miles had smiled at him and said he could spend whatever he felt was reasonable. That was a dangerous thing to say to Charlie, whose talents had never included handling money well, but he gave himself a stern order to not overspend.

He was doing really well, until he discovered Target had already discounted its holiday supplies. But since no one in the whole freaking house even owned so much a Christmas ornament between them, they couldn't fault him for spending a little more, right? After all, they had a big house to decorate. He'd do everything stylish, in specific colors, and it would look magnificent.

Charlie was in his bedroom, finishing putting on his lipstick, when Miles called for him. "Charlie, love, there's a delivery for you."

Yay, his Target delivery was here! He hurried to the front door, where the UPS guy was stacking box after box near the door. Charlie frowned. Were they all for him? That couldn't be, could it?

The guy dropped another long box. Ah, that was the tree, Charlie saw. He'd picked a large one that would stand beautifully in the living room.

"That's it. I counted them out," the guy said.

He waved in a friendly gesture and climbed back into his truck. Miles looked at the boxes, a puzzled expression on his face. "What's all this?" he asked. "Did you get a head start on Christmas shopping?"

Charlie smiled at him. "In a way. This is the Christmas deco stuff I ordered. I told you."

Miles's frown deepened. "You said you'd buy a tree and some ornaments. This looks like you bought half the store."

"It was all on sale," Charlie said. "Buy one get one half off."

"Hmm," Miles said, and Charlie didn't feel like he appreciated what a good deal that was. "Let's get it all inside and see what you got."

"Oh, Christmas decorations," Josh said as he helped bring the boxes inside. "What did you get?"

"I chose everything in blue, white, and silver. Wait till you see the tree," Charlie said, feeling giddy at the thought of revealing it. "It's massive and it will look perfect here."

But when he unpacked all the boxes, Miles's frown seemed to deepen. Instead of enthusiasm, he hung back while Josh and Indy praised Charlie for his choices and started to set up the tree. He could understand why Brad didn't give a shit, though even he tried to say something nice. And Connor and Noah were excused as well. But why didn't Miles show even a shred of appreciation?

And then he remembered, the little detail Miles had confessed about hating the holidays. He missed his parents and his sister, who'd all died in a boating accident years ago. Charlie's heart filled with love as he walked over to Miles, who was observing from the couch. He slipped onto his lap and hugged him.

"I'm sorry you miss them," he said, confirmed in his line of reasoning when Miles buried his head against Charlie. Around them, the room grew quiet.

"I miss them so fucking much this time of year," he said, and Charlie heard the emotion in his voice. "My dad would buy the biggest natural tree he could find and my mom would decorate it with us. Every year, she'd add the sorry attempts at Christmas ornaments Belinda, my sister, and I would make in school. They were awful, but she always hung them."

Charlie wished he had a memory like that, but his own mother hadn't given a shit about him or anything he did in school. And even less after she'd started suspecting he was gay. He pushed the memory down. Now was not the time. Besides, Christmas didn't hold specific negative memories for him, not like it did for Miles.

"Do you still have them?" he asked. Miles wouldn't have thrown them out, would he?

"Yeah, they're in a box in the garage. I haven't looked at them since I packed them, many years ago."

"We should put them up," Josh said softly. "So you can

remember them in love. I don't have anything like that from my childhood."

"Me neither," Indy said. "We had Christmas trees a few times, but nothing personal like that."

"I'm sure my mom kept all my craft projects," Connor said with a laugh. "They're probably in a box somewhere in her house. She never threw anything out."

"I've got a box from my mom," Noah said. "My dad gave it to me a while ago, said he wouldn't use it anyway."

"Bring them in," Indy said. 'If you want to. I agree with Josh that it would be lovely to honor your loved ones like that."

With a little digging, Noah and Miles both found their boxes in the garage. Both were organized and had all their boxes neatly labeled, which made Charlie laugh. It was a good thing he had nothing in storage, because it would've taken him ages to find anything. Hell, he lost his phone half the time.

Noah had decorations his mother had bought, old-fashioned ornaments made of glass and various angels. And Miles unpacked a load of clumsily crafted ornaments he and his sister had made. One was a little foam Christmas tree with a picture of a young Miles.

"That was fourth grade, I think," Miles said.

"God, you were cute," Charlie said.

"*Were*," Brad repeated with a cheeky grin, which made Miles smile.

"Careful, brat. Or we'll find out how cute you look with your ass all red."

"Yes, Daddy," Brad said, but his eyes laughed as much as Miles's.

They put the tree up and hung the ornaments. When it was done, it looked nothing like the modern, stylish tree in silver, blue, and white Charlie had imagined, but they all agreed it was perfection.

FIVE DAYS AFTER THE WEDDING, Indy was still basking in the afterglow. It had been picture-perfect, their intimate gathering, and the wedding night one for the books. The ceremony shouldn't have made a difference, but it did.

Indy held out his hand, studying the gorgeous ring Noah and Connor had surprised him and Josh with. They'd been sneaky, those two, making their own little plans, but Indy loved it. Indy had blinked when he'd seen all four names in the engraving. He'd expected his and Noah's names, or maybe his in the middle and Josh's on the other side, but Connor's had been added too. It had surprised him, and yet it hadn't, this proof of how their relationship was still evolving.

Even now he sensed it, as Connor and Noah were in the bathroom together, showering after a workout. Before, they would've waited their turn, even if they didn't care much about seeing each other naked. But they'd grown closer, and it showed in little things. He and Josh couldn't be more excited, since it made things so much easier.

"Admiring your bling?" Miles asked with a laugh.

Indy dragged his eyes away from his hand and smiled. "Very much."

"It's gorgeous," Charlie said, snuggled up against Miles, flipping through a fashion magazine. "Didn't Noah and Connor want rings for themselves?"

Indy shook his head. "No. Noah has an aversion to any kind of metal on his body after his accident. It feels restrictive to him. He wore his dog tags for a long time, but he took those off a few months back. And because of that, Connor decided it would be better if it was only me and Josh who wore them. It's their wedding gift to us."

"That's beautiful," Charlie sighed.

They looked at the door when Brad walked in, his face showing he'd had a rough day. Still, he hung his jacket on the right hook, deposited his shoes and his backpack in the right place, and greeted them all. Max got an extended belly rub before Brad sought out his boyfriends. Charlie scooted over, making space for Brad, who settled next to him on the couch with a deep sigh.

"Bad day, sweetheart?" Miles asked, his hand finding Brad's head and stroking it.

"Yeah. Nothing big, but I'm tired, Daddy."

They hadn't talked about it much, but Indy knew Burke's return had affected Brad. Indy was proud of him for taking a stand and being open about his relationship with Miles and Charlie. That couldn't have been easy for Brad, who was so sensitive to rejection.

"Do you want me to draw you a nice bath so you can relax a little?" Miles asked.

Before Brad could answer, a phone rang with an unfamiliar ringtone. Indy froze.

The new DA had provided him with a burner phone. No one else had that number, they assured him. Indy had appreciated the gesture, even if he was a little freaked out that a measure like this was still necessary after Duncan had died. The phone had remained silent, except for an occasional text. But now that phone was ringing, the ringtone shrill and on a frequency that made his head hurt.

He picked it up quickly, his stomach swirling uncomfortably. Across from him, Miles tensed, gesturing at Charlie to go get someone. Noah and Connor, Indy guessed.

"Hello?" Indy said.

"Please provide the verification code given to you with this phone," a detached, female voice spoke.

Indy blurted out the four-digit code they'd agreed upon and that he'd memorized.

"Please hold for Mr. Dwyer," the woman said.

The DA himself was calling. This was not good. Connor came hurrying in, still shirtless, and took a seat next to him. Without hesitating, he reached for Indy's hand. Indy was glad for the comfort the sensation of that big, strong hand provided.

"I'm sorry to disturb you at home, Indy, but I've received some worrisome news I wanted to share with you."

If nothing else, Indy appreciated the directness of the new DA. This man wasted no time on chitchat or polite conversation but went straight to the point.

"What happened?" Indy asked.

"The FBI has informed us they have received credible threats against you. They've been monitoring the chatter of several operatives within the Fitzpatrick organization. Things were quiet after Duncan Fitzpatrick was killed and most of the organization was in disarray, but lately, they have picked up renewed chatter. The pattern that's emerging is that there is a new leadership rising within the organization, and some of these leaders are determined to prevent you from testifying."

Indy swallowed back the bile that had risen in his throat. "What do you mean by credible threats?"

Even through the phone, he heard Dwyer letting out a deep sigh. "I'm so sorry, Indy, but there's a renewed contract on your head. The reward is nowhere near as high as it was previously, but still high enough to attract unsavory characters. The good news is that so far, there's little concrete information they have on you, and it doesn't seem like your address has been leaked, but the FBI fears that if they take long enough, they will find you. I really want to urge you again to accept our offer of placing you in a safe house."

A new contract. Indy closed his eyes, trying to process what the DA was telling him. Would this nightmare never end? He thought he'd be free after Duncan died, after Connor had taken down so many of the leaders in the Fitzpatrick organization. They should've known there was too much money to be made from the drug trade for the whole organization to collapse. Someone new would always rise to the top.

And he was the biggest threat to sending a whole bunch of their leaders to prison for a long time. Even with all the other evidence they had, the DA had assured Indy that his testimony was crucial. He was the only one who could provide a first-person witness account of the daily operations of the Fitzpatricks.

"The contract," he asked, forcing himself to stay calm. "Is it dead or alive?"

"It's a kill contract, Indy. They're no longer interested in taking you alive."

"Well, at least that's good news," Indy said, and he didn't realize how true that was until he had uttered those words.

His biggest fear had never been dying. It had always been to be taken alive and tortured to death. Or worse, to be taken alive and forced to do the will of his captors because they would take his loved ones. Noah. Josh. Connor. Miles and his boys. Indy had so many more weak spots now than before. A kill contract was good news, since it meant they were only after him.

"Our offer of a safe house stands. We can relocate you anywhere in the country, and as I assured you before, we're willing to allow you to bring your partner with you. Pardon me, partners. We understand your relationship is unconventional, and we're willing to accommodate. Please understand, Indy, that your safety is a big concern for us. We want to win the case, but it's also because we don't want to see you or your loved ones harmed."

Indy wasn't sure if the man was speaking the truth about the latter part. He sounded sincere, but then again, he was a politician of some sorts, wasn't he? Indy had never met a politician who couldn't lie through his teeth and make it sound like the sincerest compliment ever.

What he did know, because Miles had told him as much, was that the offer for a safe spot not just for him but for Noah, Josh, and Connor as well was extraordinary. If nothing else, it indicated the value of Indy's testimony. That didn't mean he was tempted in the least to accept the offer. Not even after what the DA had just told him.

"Mr. Dwyer, I appreciate you telling me this. Believe me, I understand the gravity of the situation. But understand where I'm coming from. I have done nothing but run for the last two years, and I'm done. I can't run anymore. I have to take a stand. That means I'm staying home, with my loved ones, with my family."

Dwyer sighed again. "I was afraid that would be your answer. I understand, Indy, but I really urge you to reconsider. And if the prospect of a safe house is too much for you, please allow us to place a permanent protection detail on you and your partners. We want to make sure you're safe."

Indy thought about it. The idea of having strangers around him, federal agents, was almost as bad as going to a safe house. It would mean a total loss of privacy, not just for him, but for all of them. It would affect Josh's PTSD for sure, and it would be an impediment of their lifestyle, including the interactions between Miles and his boys. What would happen if Brad had an off day? Or if Josh needed a heavy session? How on earth could they pull that off with federal agents watching them?

No, if they needed protection, they'd have to go the route Noah and Connor had suggested and hire private security, men they could vet and trust. Men they could choose based on their understanding of their unconventional relationship, as Dwyer had formulated it so politely.

"Thank you, but I'll need to think about this. Quite frankly, my experiences with the FBI and cops haven't been all that good, as you know from reading my file. Plus, even having federal agents around would be a massive breach of our privacy. I will discuss it with my partners, and I'll let you know. I doubt we'll take you up on your offer, but I think we will consider hiring private security."

Dwyer was silent for a few beats. "Indy, can I speak frankly?" he asked, his voice dropping to a low level. "And by frankly, I mean that this conversation stays between us, or at least between me and you and your partners?"

Indy cocked an eyebrow. Where was the man going with this? "Sure."

"This is off the record, and you're at no obligation to accept it, but my brother runs a security firm, and he might be able to provide you with the security you need right now."

"Okay," Indy said slowly, not understanding why the man needed to be this secretive about something like this. "That's good to know."

"He's not only superb at what he does, and he can provide you with plenty of references to back up that claim, but I think he would also be a good fit considering your lifestyle. He's a Dom, Indy. An experienced, trained Dom. You need not tell me anything as this is far outside the scope of my investigation, but from the hints I read in your file, it seems like at least some members of your household may be involved in a BDSM lifestyle. My brother wouldn't bat an eye. He would allow you the freedom to keep on doing whatever it is you're doing. You don't need to confirm or deny this, but I can give you his contact information if you're interested."

Indy grinned despite it all. Wasn't that a surprise, to find out that the somewhat straight-laced DA had a kinky brother like that? "It sounds like he would be a good fit for us, sir, thank you. I'd appreciate his contact information."

This time, Dwyer's sigh was one of relief that was easy to spot. "Excellent. Thank you for considering it, for considering him. It would make me feel better too, to know he's protecting you. It sounds like a horrible cliché, Indy, but I do worry about you."

"Thank you," Indy said. "It sounds like a horrible cliché as well, but I do appreciate it."

"My brother's name is Wander Dwyer, and I will text his contact info to your burner phone. Please use that phone to contact him."

After hanging up, Indy looked at Connor. "Did you get most of that?"

Connor nodded. "Yeah. A private security guy who's a Dom, huh? That could prove interesting."

8

Wander Dwyer was not at all what Connor had expected. He wasn't sure why, but when he'd heard Wander was a Dom, he'd imagined someone with a build much like his own. Instead, Wander was almost a head shorter, bald with a neatly trimmed beard and a toned body with a tight build that showed even in his cargo pants and a shirt that hugged his muscles.

His handshake was firm, and he met Connor's gaze with a pair of sharp, assessing brown eyes. "Nice to meet you, Connor."

Connor observed him as he went around the room, introducing himself to everyone. They all got the same firm handshake, the intentional look that signaled steel wrapped in a thin layer of friendliness. He even kneeled to greet Max, the dog sniffing him before deciding he wasn't worth the bother.

Connor wasn't sure how the man pulled it off, but he exuded a self-confidence that told you not to fuck with him. It was funny, but in a way, it reminded him of Indy. It was that core of titanium that showed, even if the outside of Indy was a lot less intimidating than this Wander-guy.

Indy had insisted they all meet with him, including Charlie and Brad. He wanted everyone to be comfortable with the presence of the security guys, and if that didn't say everything about his character, Connor didn't know what would.

Connor had assumed Wander would start with explaining how he planned to protect them, but instead, he looked at Indy and said, "Tell me how you envision this."

Indy's eyes widened in surprise before he caught himself. "Well, if I can be absolutely frank with you..."

"I would much prefer that," Wander said. "We'll be spending a lot of time in each other's company, and that will go a lot smoother if we can be honest with each other."

Indy nodded, signaling his approval. "Okay, then. I had not envisioned this at all. In fact, I dislike the very fact you're here, and the idea you'll be around for as long as the trial takes is not something I'm looking forward to."

Connor almost held his breath, curious to see how Wander would react to this display of Indy's frustration.

"I can understand. As glamorous as having private security may seem to some people, the reality is it's a fucking nuisance. I get that. So let's talk about how we can make this work for you and for your family."

The man had just earned major points with Connor by using the word *family*. One look at Indy's face showed Indy shared Connor's assessment.

"I think the most important thing for all of us is privacy," Indy said. "We want to live our lives undisturbed as much as possible."

"I understand, but now I have to be honest with you. That's not gonna happen. If you want to keep yourself and your family safe, we'll need to adjust your schedules, your routines, and your daily lives. That being said, I can't guarantee you privacy, but I can assure you of a complete lack of judgment."

Indy cocked his head, looking at Wander with curiosity. "What do you mean by a lack of judgment?"

Wander leaned back in his chair, looking around the room. "Complete honesty, yeah?"

Indy nodded.

Wander pointed at Connor. "You're a Dom, and Josh is your sub." He pointed at Miles next. "You're dominant as well, but just with Brad. A different kind of dominant, though. I'm guessing you're his daddy? And while Charlie might look like a sub, he's anything but, considering the way he interacts with you and Brad. Brad, however, is a true sub, one that aims to please everyone."

Connor followed the casual assessment with rising admiration. How had the man pegged all of them so quickly?

"Then there's you, Indy. You're with Noah, who may look like a Dom, but isn't. And you yourself are the farthest thing from submissive. On the other hand, there's definitely something between you and Josh, so if I had to take a guess, I would say the four of you are together, if not for the fact Noah and Connor may not have worked out the specifics of their relationship yet."

Connor's mouth dropped open. What the fuck was the guy suggesting, that he and Noah were together? What the hell did he base that on?

Wander crossed his arms in front of his chest. "How did I do?"

Connor couldn't help it. "He and Josh are together. There's nothing between me and Noah."

He caught meaningful eye contact between Indy and Josh he didn't like at all. At least Noah agreed with him, as he sent Connor a look of approval for speaking up and correcting the security guy.

"I'd say that was spot on," Indy said, ignoring Connor's correction. "So now you understand why we need our privacy. This is not something we can turn off for a few months."

Wander's eyes traveled to Josh as he said, "I agree, and please don't, as this may have negative consequences. Hence my remark that while I may not be able to guarantee you privacy, what I can assure you of is a complete lack of judgment. Both me and my men are used to a wide range of lifestyles, relationships, and kinks. Trust me, we've seen it all, and we don't judge. We won't intervene, we won't comment, and we'd never try to discourage you."

Indy leaned forward. "But you'll still be there, watching us."

Something stirred in Connor, a flash of an image. Him, dominating Josh, whipping him, fucking him, with Wander watching. Why did that idea turn him on so much? He was oh so grateful he never blushed when Wander's eyes found his, and a hint of a smile played on the man's lips.

"Yes, we may be watching. Not necessarily in your bedroom, but if your activities take place in common areas of the house, there will be times when we'll be there. That may not necessarily be a negative thing for all of you, though, can I point that out?"

Both Indy and Josh looked at Connor, and he suppressed a sigh. Really, did they have to be that obvious about it?

"True," Indy admitted with a sly smile. "So from what you're saying, I gather your men are all Doms as well?"

"No. Some of them are, but I also have subs on my team and a few involved in other lifestyles and kinks. Most of them are gay or bi, but there are also a few straight guys who simply don't care. But all of them are carefully vetted and selected for their tolerance, acceptance, and discretion. I've done a lot of security work for celebrities involved in a kinky lifestyle, and that's why it's almost become a prerequisite to have experience in this if you want to work for me." He shrugged. "It wasn't what I had set out to achieve with my firm, but I can't deny there is a demand for security personnel who have experience with a range of lifestyles."

"But you're a Dom?" Indy asked.

"Yes."

Connor liked that the man didn't feel the need to explain himself, let alone defend himself.

"Do you have a sub right now? Or a partner? Because that might get complicated with an assignment like this," Indy said, and Connor suppressed a grin. It was incredible Indy would worry about the man's personal life, minutes after meeting him. It was such a classic gesture for Indy, always trying to look out for everyone.

Wander seemed to understand the intention behind the question. "Not at the moment. I belong to a club where I participate regularly, but I don't have a partner or a permanent sub right now. It's a tough combination with my job, I've discovered."

"Okay," Indy said. A range of emotions flashed over his face before he let out a sigh. "I guess this is the best solution under these circumstances. Can you please explain to us what your protection would look like?"

For the next ten minutes, Wander went through a series of questions with them all, then explained he would need more information for a detailed plan, but that he proposed to have at least three men present. That was kind of what Connor and Miles had figured out as well when they'd discussed it, so Connor was glad to see Wander arrive at the same conclusion.

"Where will you and your men stay?" Noah asked.

"If you agree to hire my team, I'd prefer to stay inside the house myself, preferably on this couch. That will give me a good spot to keep an eye on things, even at night. My men will rotate shifts, and we'll book a motel nearby for them when they're off-shift."

Noah nodded. "That would work for us."

After making sure there were no pressing questions, Wander said, "Would it be possible for me to speak with just Noah, Connor, and Miles? I have something I want to talk about to them."

Indy was clearly surprised, but after a quick look at Noah, he agreed.

"Let's step outside for a minute," Noah suggested.

Once outside, Connor shot Wander a questioning glance. "What is this about?"

"I wanted to be clear about our roles," Wander said, looking from Connor to Noah and then to Miles.

Miles apparently understood what he was referring to before Connor and Noah. "You want to avoid a pissing match," he said.

"Yes. We need to make something crystal clear. You were an FBI agent." He pointed at Miles. "And from what I understand, a damn good one. You're a decorated war hero," he said to Noah. "My sense is you're kind of the man of the house, so to speak. And you're a decorated Marine with a stellar career in law enforcement."

That last part was aimed at Connor, who appreciated

Wander had done his research before showing up for his appointment here.

"Aside from the fact you each have qualifications to lead, there is enough testosterone between the three of you to light a fire. So, we need to make clear who's in charge. That would be me. When shit goes down, I have to trust the three of you to follow my orders. There can be no questioning, no second-guessing, no following your own plans."

As much as Connor resented it, he understood. The resentment was all on him, a simple case of his pride being hurt a little for acknowledging someone else as his boss. But Wander was right. If they entrusted the security of their family to him, they would have to let him make the decisions.

"On the other hand, I will in no way infringe upon your role as dominants or daddies or whatever the fuck it is you're doing. It may be intimidating to have someone else watch, a stranger and a Dom to boot, and from what I understand, it's not something you guys are used to. So I promise to stay out of your personal relationships and power dynamics, unless you ask me for advice."

Ask him for advice? Huh, Connor thought, there was an interesting concept. If the man was as experienced as he seemed, maybe they could even learn a thing or two from him.

"Sounds reasonable," Noah said. "And I think we can all agree on the necessity of a clear chain of command with you at the top."

"Good. Glad to hear it. Now, which one of you do I talk to when I have concerns or questions?"

Noah and Connor looked at each other, and Connor wasn't even sure how he knew what Noah was thinking, but he did. "Miles," they said in unison.

Miles's eyes widened.

"You have the most experience in this," Connor said, clamping a hand on the man's shoulder. "That's all that matters."

Wander shot them a look that seemed a hell of a lot like approval, and Noah grinned at him. "We're not that hard to get along with."

"Don't start telling lies now, Flint," Connor told him. "We both know you're a pain in the ass."

Wander smiled. "A pain in the ass, huh? The good kind or the bad kind?"

9

B rad loved being home during the weekends. As much as he liked his job and enjoyed spending time with his students, he couldn't deny it was demanding. By the time the weekend came around, he was usually more than ready for it. And since Miles never worked on the weekends and Charlie often worked either Saturday or Sunday, it was a perfect time for Brad to get extra one-on-one time with his daddy. This time it was different, however.

It wasn't that the presence of the three security guards or whatever they were supposed to call them bothered Brad. Hell, he'd always had a fetish for sex in public, so strangers watching while he performed sexual acts was more a turn-on than a nuisance. But it did bother his daddy.

Brad didn't know if it was because Miles didn't want them to know about his condition, because he was embarrassed, or because he simply wanted to keep sex private, but after a few days with Wander and his men, Brad was about to explode with sexual frustration. And those had been weekdays, mornings and evenings only.

Sure, he still got his daily fix of sucking Daddy off, but it wasn't the same when he had to do it quickly in the bedroom rather than being able to take his time and do it in public. There was something so satisfying about dropping to his knees in front of everybody and taking care of his daddy. Call him weird or perverted, but he loved sucking his daddy off while the man was doing something else. It made him feel used, like all he was good for was sucking that cock. Or taking it up his ass, which was also fine by him. But now all of a sudden, his daddy had become all proper in public, and Brad didn't like it one bit.

At least Daddy still remembered to give him his daily morning spankings, though even those were in private and a hell of a lot quieter. Brad sighed miserably, sitting on the couch with his arms crossed in front of him, staring at the wall. Life sucked right now.

Charlie was at work, and Noah and Connor were in the kitchen, involved in a deep conversation with Daddy about fuck knows what. And judging by the sounds, Indy and Josh were taking a bath together. A bath with benefits. Brad recognized Indy's soft giggle, a clear indication he was teasing Josh in some sexual way.

And dammit, Brad was bored out of his mind. He'd been sitting on this damn couch for an hour, snuggling with Max. He needed something to do, preferably something with Daddy. It had been hours since his last release, so Daddy had to be desperate by now, right? Maybe he could give him a hint he was willing to take care of it. You could say what you wanted, but Daddy was adept at reading Brad's signals.

He got up from the couch and, after a quick look at Wander, who was positioned on a chair near the front door, walked into the kitchen. He only needed to listen for a few seconds to know that conversation would bore him out of his mind. It was something about how the body dealt with trauma. Undoubtedly a stimulating topic for those three, but not something Brad had any intention of engaging in, especially not during a weekend.

He quietly made his way over to Daddy and put his mouth near his ear. "Do you need me, Daddy?"

Daddy patted his leg absentmindedly, never even looking at him. "Thank you, sweetheart, but I took care of it myself. I'm good for now. Go do something for yourself. Enjoy your time off."

He took care of it himself? Since when had that become a thing when Brad was home? Inside Brad, it stormed, but he bit his lip and walked away. He couldn't throw a tantrum now, not with Wander in the room. Daddy would get so upset if he pulled a stunt like that. He'd asked Brad to be on his best behavior while they had guests, and even though Brad didn't always succeed in obeying Daddy, he sure tried. Being punished by Daddy wasn't fun, whereas being rewarded for good behavior usually meant he would spend a few hours taking care of him and Charlie both. So he sucked it up and retreated into their bedroom, where he had more privacy, Max on his heels.

He woke up disoriented, Max still snoring at his feet, then realized he'd fallen asleep while watching TV. A quick check of the clock told him he'd slept for almost two hours. Huh, he'd been more tired than he had realized. Or more bored, which was a plausible explanation as well. Either way, Daddy had to be dying for relief, right?

He got up, dragged a quick hand through his hair and hurried to where he heard voices. He found all of them in the living room, except for Charlie, who hadn't returned from work yet. Indy was telling Wander the story of how he'd kicked Daddy's ass back in Kansas. Brad loved that story, even if he always felt a little sorry for Daddy. People tended to underestimate Indy, because he looked like a fucking elf and yet was deadly in jiu jitsu.

He found his favorite spot, kneeling at Daddy's feet, in the perfect position to suck him off. More out of habit than anything else, he looked up at him and asked for permission with his eyes. But Daddy shook his head, and something inside Brad froze oh so cold. What had he done wrong that Daddy didn't want him to take care of him anymore? Had he messed up somehow without realizing?

He sat back, leaning against the couch rather than Daddy's legs, and went over every interaction they'd had in the past week, trying to look at it from every angle to see where he'd gotten it wrong. But no matter how hard he tried, he couldn't come up with one incident where he'd disobeyed Daddy. He'd been so good this week, so why was Daddy rejecting him? As he sat at his Daddy's feet, painfully missing the usual affectionate hand on his neck or on his head, he realized the truth.

This wasn't because of him. He had done nothing wrong. This was because of Daddy. This was Miles having issues of some kind. Miles had distanced himself from Brad for whatever reason, most likely because of Wander's presence or that of his men. Embarrassment was the most logical explanation, but was it embarrassment over his own condition or over Brad? Was his daddy ashamed of him? Of the relationship they had?

His face hardened. If that was the case, what was he still doing here? Why was he offering to take care of a man who was embarrassed to even be seen with him? Hell, he'd affirmed their relationship in front of Burke, and this was how Miles treated him when it was his turn?

Brad blinked, his heart filling with resolve. He was better

than this, worth more than this. He slowly rose and in the midst of Indy's story, he spoke up.

"Come find me when you've found your balls," he said to Miles, his voice ice cold.

The conversation came to an immediate halt, and all faces turned toward him, including Wander's.

"My balls?" Miles asked, his voice hesitant.

Brad raised his chin. "Yes, your balls. The ones you need to stop feeling fucking ashamed of me, of us. Tell me when you've found them."

"Brad! What the hell, boy?" Miles burst out, jumping up from the couch and facing Brad.

Brad stabbed a finger in his chest. "No, you don't get to *boy* me after basically ignoring me for a week."

"You need to watch your tone. You know better than to talk to me like this."

Brad let out a scathing laugh. "Listen to yourself! Even now you can't be yourself. You sound like a fucking wannabe, not like my daddy. What the fuck is wrong with you? Why are you such a fucking prude all of a sudden? Why won't you let me take care of you?"

The tears that formed in his eyes angered him, and he wiped them off with a violent gesture. "I deserve more than this. We had an understanding, an agreement of how our relationship works. If you don't hold up your end of the bargain, well, then neither do I. You can go fuck yourself for all I care."

He didn't wait for Miles's reaction, but stormed to the front door, where he yanked his winter coat off the rack. He whistled at Max, who came trotting toward the door instantly.

In a flash, Wander was in front of him. "Where are you going?"

Brad met his steely look with icy indifference. "None of your fucking business. Your job is to protect Indy and his men. Clearly, I'm not one of them, so get the fuck out of my way."

It seemed those words finally triggered Miles into action, and with a few big steps, he stood in front of Brad, pushing Wander aside. But it wasn't Daddy Miles or even a shadow of him. It was a humbled, shaken Miles.

"Brad, please, don't go. Please. Stay."

"Why?"

Miles took a small step toward him. "So I can apologize? Because I love you. Because you love me, even when I'm an ass?"

Brad swallowed. "Are all of those questions or statements?"

"Statements. I fucked up, Brad. God, I'm so sorry. I was..."

"Embarrassed," Brad supplied, his voice filled with bitterness. "You were embarrassed of me, of what we have together."

"No, not like this. Well, a little, maybe, but it's not the whole picture."

Brad crossed his arms again, determined not to surrender quite that easily, even if the wounded look on Miles's face got to him. He couldn't stand to see him hurting. "Then paint the picture for me."

Miles sent a pained look sideways toward Wander. Then he refocused on Brad, his eyes soft and apologetic. "This is on me, Brad. I was insecure, scared that Wander and his men would judge me for my relationship with you and Charlie, but mostly with you."

"Because I'm such a slut?" Brad had to ask it, had to know if that was the reason.

"No, sweetheart, I swear. Because of me, of how much I

need you, how much I use you. I was afraid they would think I was selfish, using you and not giving enough in return."

Brad frowned. "But I like to be used. I don't understand."

"I know you do, but they don't know that, and I feared they would think I was being indifferent or mean to you."

Brad scoffed. "You realize that makes no sense at all, right? The way you've treated me the last week, *that's* being indifferent and mean. I need you, Daddy, as much as you need me, and I don't give a flying fuck what anyone else thinks."

From the corner of his eye, he caught Wander grinning. That at least was something, to know the man understood where he was coming from.

Miles gave him a tight smile. "I forget sometimes how wise you are, my sweet boy."

Brad moved forward until their faces were only inches apart. "I was ashamed of myself for such a long time, and I can't go back to that. Now that I've finally found freedom in being me, I can't go back to pretending to be something and someone I'm not. If you want to be with me, you'll have to make that stand with me. No more running, Daddy. This is who we are."

10
_____

That night, Miles couldn't sleep. Usually, he was out like a light, especially when both his boys made a little extra effort to wear him out—like they'd done tonight. He was so sated after fucking both of them that his cock had been quiet now for hours. But his head hadn't been.

He'd fucked up. Big time.

He still couldn't believe he'd been that stupid, that superficial, that he'd valued the opinion of others over the well-being and love of his boys. Well, Brad especially. He'd rejected him, denied him, all because he'd been scared of being judged. And that, after Brad had so courageously gone public about their relationship in front of his brother. The thought left a bitter taste in Miles's mouth all over again.

He'd always prided himself on being true to himself, about not hiding who he was. Apparently, he hadn't been quite as proud and accepting of himself and his relationship as he'd claimed to be. What the hell had happened? How had he allowed himself to feel ashamed of the single most important thing in his life—his relationship with Charlie and Brad?

He'd made Brad feel like he'd been ashamed of him, of who Brad was and how he took care of Miles, and that was a bitter pill to swallow. He'd vowed to do right by his boy, but he'd failed him. Spectacularly.

"Can't sleep?" Brad's soft voice interrupted his thoughts. He was nestled against Miles with Charlie on Brad's other side. Miles found Brad's eyes focused on him.

"I thought you were asleep," Miles said softly.

"I was, but something woke me up and then I felt the tension in your body."

Brad didn't ask what was keeping Miles up, and he appreciated him not rubbing it in, because he had to know what was bothering Miles. "I failed you."

Brad let out a soft sigh, then curled up against Miles. "Yes," he said, his breath wafting over Miles's naked chest. Miles smiled. It was such a classic Brad move, to not mince his words but affirm the truth.

"I'm sorry," Miles said.

"You've apologized already."

Miles sighed. "I know, but it doesn't feel like it's enough."

"I've forgiven you," Brad stated.

"Have you really? I can't help but fear I've lost your trust."

"You know what you always tell me when I've been bad, right? That once I've had my punishment, I'm forgiven and everything is good between us."

Miles considered the truth of that statement. "And you really feel like everything is okay again after that?"

"Yeah, because you keep assuring me it is, Daddy. You punish me and then it's in the past."

Miles kissed his head. Out of the mouths of babes, the

saying went, and Brad was proving it. "I love you so much. I'm sorry if I ever made you doubt that."

"I love you too, Daddy," Brad said, his voice sounding sleepy.

"Go back to sleep, sweetheart," he said, then kissed his head again.

As Brad's breathing evened out, then slowed down, Miles's head still spun. Brad had made it sound so easy, letting go and forgiving himself, but how did he do that? They'd told Charlie what had happened, and he'd been shocked, too. Charlie had fully chosen Brad's side in this, which was the right thing to do, but it made Miles feel even more shitty.

Charlie hadn't been angry with him, but there had been tension between them, the residue of his emotions over Brad getting hurt. How could he ever forgive himself for hurting his boys like this, for failing as their daddy, their lover and boyfriend?

When half an hour later he still couldn't sleep, he crawled out of bed and left their room. Maybe watching some mindless TV would help—with the headphones on. He'd forgotten all about Wander until the man spoke up.

"Trouble sleeping?"

Miles barely kept himself from jumping. "Fucking hell, you scared the bejeezus out of me."

He made out Wander's form on the couch, then remembered he'd stated that's where he'd sleep. A light sleeper, he'd called himself. Well, that turned out to be accurate.

"Sorry. I wanted to say something before you plonked down on the couch and landed in my lap."

Wander swung his legs sideways and sat up, and Miles lowered himself into a chair. "I appreciate the sentiment."

Wander flicked on a light, and Miles blinked a few times

to let his eyes adjust. He waited for Wander to say something, but when the man stayed quiet, Miles added, "And yes, I had trouble sleeping."

"Your boys still upset with you?"

Miles shook his head. "No. I'm upset with myself. I always tell Brad that once I've punished him, he's forgiven, but I'm having trouble applying my own wisdom."

Wander smiled at him. "Have you received your punishment then?"

Miles stared at him and lightning struck his brain. How the hell did the man pinpoint the problem so easily? Of course Miles was having trouble forgiving himself. He'd never received his punishment. It was so simple and yet he'd never considered it.

"How did you know?" he asked Wander, who shrugged.

"It's not that hard to determine. Charlie may not be a sub, but he's way too tenderhearted to ever punish you, and Brad wouldn't even think of it. You're his daddy, so punishing you isn't even an option in his world."

Damn, the guy was perceptive. "So where does that leave me?"

Wander leaned forward in his seat, resting his arms on his legs. "Can I ask you a personal question? Feel free to say no."

Miles almost laughed at how absurd it was that the man would ask for permission after what he'd seen from them already, but fuck if he didn't appreciate it. "Sure."

He had a suspicion what the topic would be, and Wander didn't disappoint. "You have some kind of medical issue?"

"Yes. I could give you the medical spiel, but the bottom line is that I'm almost constantly aroused."

"Damn. That's hella inconvenient."

Miles let out a breath of relief at that easy acceptance. "Yes. Even more before I met Brad and Charlie and moved in here. I've found a true home here where I can be myself without judgment."

"I can see that. It's a special group, these men."

Miles's heart surged with pride that he was part of this. "It is. I was one of Indy's FBI agents when he was in protective custody. He saved my life, then saved my life in another sense by introducing me to Brad and taking me in. I owe him everything."

Wander smiled, leaning back in his seat again. "He's a fascinating one. So pretty on the outside, a cute little twink, but the kid's got balls the size of Texas."

"He does."

Wander's face tightened. "My brother told me the chatter is increasing. They mean business."

"No wonder. Indy's the single biggest threat to what's left of the Fitzpatricks. With his testimony, your brother can take them all down." Miles thought of something. "Please tell me your brother is under protection as well."

"He is," Wander assured him. "But if you'll forgive me being blunt: the DA is replaceable, Indy is not. Killing my brother would only mean postponing the trial. Killing Indy is the end of the case."

Miles had to agree with that logic. "Still, wouldn't you rather protect him?" He realized the fault in his reasoning as soon as he said it and could've slapped himself. "No, of course not. You're much too close to him."

"You need a certain amount of objectivity, though it's hard. Since my team often does longer-term assignments, we do tend to get attached to our protectees."

There was a hint of a smile around his mouth. "Like me

and Indy, you mean. Yeah, I'll admit I was far from detached and professional there."

"So, your medical issue, that's where Brad comes in?" Wander reverted to the previous topic.

"He's a little slut, and I say that with all the love I have for him. He loves being used."

Wander nodded. "I figured as much. It was ballsy of him to call you out like that."

Miles's heart contracted all over again. "It was. He's a little brat, but he's my world, him and Charlie both. He needs us so much and we want nothing more than to love him and take care of him."

"They're fascinating, the dynamics here in this house," Wander said, and Miles detected a hint of emotion. "You, Charlie, and Brad...it's a hot mess in theory, but it's easy to see it works."

"When I'm not being a total ass, yes," Miles said with a small laugh.

"Then there's the other four... I can't figure out how Noah and Connor relate to each other," Wander said, and this time, there was pure curiosity in his voice.

Miles's smile widened. "You and me both. I think we're all waiting for the day those two figure out the pecking order and act on that chemistry. I mean, the sparks are there, even if they're disguised as an alpha rivalry."

"Two tops. That's never easy."

Miles hesitated. Should he tell him this? Wander was so easy to talk to, and somehow, Miles knew the man would never repeat their conversation to another soul. Plus, it wasn't like they had many secrets left. The man was a Dom anyway, and as he declared on the first day, he'd seen it all already.

"Connor bottoms occasionally for Josh or with a toy.

Noah can't. He's tried with both Josh and Indy, but it's not pleasurable for him."

"Wait... Noah and Josh? They're together as well?"

"They used to be, before Indy and Connor came into the picture. Now they're not anymore."

Wander whistled softly. "Even more complicated than I thought. It explains the easy familiarity between all of them, though. And does Noah's discomfort have anything to do with his injuries?"

"It might. As you've seen, his scars run all the way up his leg and stump. His skin is often tight, so it wouldn't be strange if he had trouble relaxing."

Wander nodded. "Makes sense."

Miles cocked his head as he studied the man. "You seem fascinated by us all," he observed.

Wander hesitated, then let out a sigh. "I'm sorry. I'm aware I've long since passed the line of the detached professional. It's just that..."

Miles waited, sensing it was Wander's turn to get personal. His face was tight with a tension Miles couldn't define, but at the same time, he looked forlorn.

"What you guys have here, it's what I've dreamed of. I know that sounds unusual, but ever since I discovered I was into D/s and kink, I've wanted to share a living situation with like-minded people so we could explore and encourage that love for kink."

At first, Miles nodded, but then he wondered. Was this an indirect way of—

"I'm not saying I want to live here," Wander hurried, probably spotting Miles's line of thought on his face. "It's not some kind of creepy, indirect way of asking to be added. Fuck no. It's more that I wondered if it was even possible, what I wanted, and then I met all of you, and it's revived that dream."

"Gotcha," Miles said. "I know I'm beyond lucky to have found these men. All I can offer is that we didn't start out this way. We started out as friends, lovers, and then found that special *click*. And Indy, he's at the heart of it all. I'm not sure you could ever replicate this dynamic intentionally with strangers."

Wander looked thoughtfully. "Good point. I guess I need to find me another Indy then."

Miles shook his head. "Impossible. He's one of a kind."

Wander raised an eyebrow. "Were you ever…?"

"Oh hell, no. Well, I might've wanted more when we first met, but Indy made it crystal clear he was Noah's, even when they were apart. Now, there's nothing more than a whole lot of love, because it's so obvious who he belongs to."

They sat for a little bit, both lost in thoughts it seemed. Then Miles yawned, his tiredness catching up with him. "I'm gonna head back in. Thanks for the talk."

"You're welcome. If I may offer one last bit of advice? Ask Connor."

Miles, who had already risen from his seat, frowned. "Connor? For what?"

"To dole out your punishment so you can let go."

11

W hen Miles calmly told them that morning he felt he needed to be punished for how he'd treated Brad, Charlie's mouth dropped open a little.

"P-punished?" he stuttered. "How? Why?"

Brad looked shocked at first as well, but then understanding bloomed in his eyes. Charlie still didn't get it, though. Why would Miles need punishment? He'd apologized to Brad, hadn't he? Didn't that mean everything was okay now? Charlie understood Miles had hurt Brad and agreed he'd behaved like an ass, but once he'd apologized, it was done. Right?

"Come sit with me," Miles said, and Charlie cuddled on his lap, Brad leaning against Miles's legs as they lounged on their bed. "Let me try and explain. If I had treated you like this and apologized, I think it would've been okay. You and I have a different dynamic than me and Brad. Because I'm his daddy, I feel like I messed up big time and that an apology won't cut it. I've damaged his trust in me, and I need to restore that. Does that make sense?"

Charlie frowned as he processed it. It sounded logical, yet at the same time it left a bitter taste in his mouth. "Does that mean it's somehow more serious when you hurt him than with me?" he asked.

"God no," Miles said, shock audible in his voice. "If that's what you heard, I did a shitty job explaining it."

"It's not that you said it, but it's kind of how it made me feel, I guess." Charlie shot Brad an apologetic look. "I know Brad needs your attention more than I do, and it's not like I'm jealous, but this feels different, like he's more worthy than I am or something."

Miles's arms tightened around him for a second before he relaxed again. "Fuck, I'm making a godawful mess of things," he said, his voice dripping with regret. "I'm so sorry, my love. I never meant to make you feel that way and I'm sorry I did. He's not more worthy than you are. I hope you know I love you both equally, in as far as you can even measure love."

That, Charlie did know. With all his heart. "I know. I really do. But then why this necessity for punishment when you hurt him and not with me?"

Miles kissed the top of his head, then said, "Brad has been hurt and disappointed by people a lot, so it's a sensitive thing with him. The way I treated him, I made him feel invisible and not good enough all over again, and considering the dynamic we have, that's a grave offense. It's shaken his trust in me as his daddy, but also my own sense of being worthy to be his daddy, if that makes sense. To restore that balance, to demonstrate to both of us that I fucked up and need to face the consequences, I think he and I both need that punishment. He needs to see my behavior has the same consequences as his, that I hold myself to the same standard if not a higher one than I do him."

Charlie let that thought play around in his head. That did make sense. It was hard for Miles to demand obedience from Brad and threaten him with punishment when his own errors didn't have consequences. "So Connor is gonna do what, spank you?"

"He might. I haven't asked him yet, but the punishment would be up to him," Miles said.

"Why Connor?" Charlie wanted to know.

"It can't be Brad, because that's not how we function, and it can't be you either, because you don't have it in you. So I needed someone else, and while Noah is kind of our *pater familias*, Connor is the disciplinarian. He's also taken over for me in disciplining Brad when I'm gone, so I figured he'd be the right choice."

"He hits hard," Brad said with awe in his voice. "The last time he spanked me for being bad, I had trouble sitting for two days."

Charlie opened his mouth, then closed it again. The thought of Miles with a red bottom was strangely satisfying. He giggled. "You may regret asking him."

Miles dipped Charlie's head so they made eye contact. "Are you laughing at me now?" he asked, his eyes sparkling.

Another giggle escaped from Charlie's lips. "Brad's right. That dude hits hard. I saw Brad's ass the last time, and it was as red as Santa's suit."

Miles shrugged, his previous worries gone from his face. "Well, that'll teach me then."

"Daddy, you don't have to do it," Brad said, suddenly sounding worried. "I appreciate the thought, but—"

"It's the right thing, sweetheart. Plus, I have the two of you to take care of me afterward, don't I?"

Brad snuggled closer, putting his head in Charlie's lap. "Thank you for doing this, Daddy."

Miles bent over and kissed Brad. "Anything for the two of you. You're my everything, you two, and don't you ever forget that."

They snuggled for a long time after that, which—of course—resulted in a blow job for Miles, and because Brad looked at him with such needy eyes, Charlie let him blow him as well. That was only fair, right?

He wasn't sure how the conversation with Connor had gone, but when Miles came back, he reported Connor was on board and that they'd do the punishment after dinner. Miles was calm, but Charlie felt a strange mix of excitement and dread. On a rational level, he understood why Miles needed to do this, but he didn't really connect with it emotionally. It was part of that dynamic he never fully got, simply because he didn't feel that way.

There were times when he'd get sad about that. Not because Miles and Brad ever excluded him, because they didn't. He was part of it as much as he chose to be. It was more that it seemed to bring Brad so much contentment, seemed to fill such a deep need, and Charlie felt at times like he was missing out on something. But then he'd realize how deeply, deeply happy he was with his men, and it would pass.

Dinner was an easy affair that day, with burgers from the new grill and a wonderful pasta salad from Josh, a new recipe that everyone declared a big success. It had grilled cheese, which Charlie hadn't even known was a thing, but it tasted delicious.

After they'd cleaned up the kitchen, done the dishes, and Charlie had helped Josh with folding a load of laundry, Connor called them into the kitchen, where all the others had already taken a seat around the table. Wander had announced he'd step outside as this was a private affair, and Charlie was glad Miles would be spared that humiliation of having a stranger observe his punishment.

"As you all know, Miles has asked me to dole out his punishment for... Well, I think he'd better explain that himself." He gestured at Miles, who rose from his chair.

"I've asked Connor to administer any punishment he'd see fit for the way I treated Brad. I denied him the privilege to serve me and ignored him, all because I felt ashamed of our relationship. In doing so, I fell short as his daddy and hurt him deeply. For that, I deserve to be disciplined."

Connor nodded. "Even though it's unusual, I agree with Miles's line of reasoning, and I've accepted my responsibility in this. Brad, how many days would you say this went on before you called him out?"

"Erm, about four days, I guess?" Brad answered.

"And how often do you usually serve him on any given day? Give us a ballpark."

Charlie could see where Connor was going with this. It was smart, linking the punishment to the offense.

"I dunno," Brad said, his voice a tad surly.

"You'd better answer me, boy, or you're gonna find yourself right next to your daddy when I paddle his ass," Connor warned him, his voice taking on that edge he had when he was in Dom mode.

Brad sat up straight. "At least five times a day, Sir. Often more."

"I think your estimate is on the conservative side, so we'll go with seven a day times four days is twenty-eight. I'll add two to make it a nice, even number, which brings us to thirty."

Miles blinked, and Charlie noticed a fine layer of sweat

breaking out on his forehead. Thirty strikes, that was going to hurt.

"That seems fair," Miles said, his voice tight.

"Good. Drop 'em and bend over." Connor was all businesslike as he pointed toward the edge of the table.

Miles got up and, without hesitation, unbuttoned his jeans and pulled them down, followed by his boxers. His cock, enthusiastic as ever when it got exposed, stood firm. Charlie's guess was that wouldn't last, since unlike Brad, Miles didn't get off on pain.

Miles sent Charlie a reassuring smile, then looked at Brad. "I love you, boy."

"I love you too, Daddy." Brad sounded emotional, and Charlie couldn't blame him as he felt the same.

Then Miles bent over, gripped the edge of the table with both hands and dropped his head low. "Ready when you are," he told Connor.

Connor didn't draw it out, the first slap with that paddle fast and secure. Charlie, who was seated almost across from where Miles was positioned, saw his man flinch at the impact. The second one followed rapidly, and at the fourth strike, he let out a grunt.

"Daddy!" Brad called out, and Noah held him back as he wanted to rise.

"He's doing this for you, Brad," Noah said, his voice warm. "He's doing this to make sure you know how much he loves you and how seriously he takes his job as your daddy."

Charlie hurried over to Brad, unable to watch the anguish on his face, and he parked himself on Brad's lap, holding him as he started crying. Miles had resorted to curses and grunts, in between gasps of breath that were close to sobs. God, the man had to hurt. Connor wasn't holding back, that paddle coming down hard.

"Please, Sir, please," Brad was now begging Connor. "It's too much."

They were at twenty now, and Connor took a break. "Do I need to stop?" he asked Miles.

"No!" Miles's reaction was a half-sob. "Just give me... I need to... Just give me a second."

Miles's body was completely tense, from his pulled-up shoulders to the tight lines of his upper body and legs.

"God, this hurts like a motherfucker," Miles let out between clenched teeth.

Connor's mouth pulled up at one side in a bit of a grin. 'Unlike Brad, you're allowed to curse at me, so have at it."

"You're a fucking sadist, you know that?" Miles spat at him.

Connor's grin grew bigger. "That should teach you to treat your boy with the respect he deserves."

"Fuck yes," Miles grumbled, then added, "Continue."

The last ten strikes were fast, but also less intense. Connor held back in a way he hadn't done before, and it made Charlie feel warm inside. Even when he was punishing Miles, Connor was still looking out for him.

"Thirty, that's it." Connor lowered his hand with the paddle. "I take it you're not gonna thank me, like my Josh always does?"

Charlie couldn't hold back a snort of laughter. Connor really was something else, wasn't he?

"Fuck you, Connor," was Miles's curt reply, spat out between grunts of pain. Charlie could see how hard he had to fight to keep himself from falling apart.

"Close enough," Connor decided. "Boys, take care of him, would you? You know what to do, Brad. You've been on the receiving end plenty enough."

Charlie slid off Brad's lap, and they came up on either

side of Miles. His ass was fiery red and already beginning to swell.

"Come on, Daddy, I'll put some of that aloe cream on it. That should help. Then a nice cooling pack, maybe?" Brad said softly, and Miles leaned on both of them as he limped to their bedroom.

Married life suited him, Connor decided. Granted, the fact that he'd taken two weeks off for the wedding and the honeymoon helped. Not that they were going anywhere. That would have to wait until it was safe for Indy to travel, but spending whole days cooped up in the house wasn't a punishment. And he was off again for Christmas and the week after.

They had sex. Lots and lots of sex. In fact, Connor tried to think of a surface they hadn't used and came up empty. He grinned as he thought of a particularly satisfying session in the kitchen with Josh braced against the refrigerator while Connor had fucked the living daylights out of him. Yup, he really did like being married.

Wander and his men were proving to be a tolerable distraction as well. Tolerable was the word that Indy had used, but if he were honest, Connor had gotten quite used to their presence and even appreciated the extra audience.

The first time he'd stripped in front of Wander had been by accident, two days after the man's arrival. Connor had woken up horny as shit after a vivid dream and had forgotten about Wander and his men. He'd walked into the living room naked, in search of Josh, and had found himself eye to eye with Wander. The man had tried to keep his composure, but as soon as his eyes had dropped down to the Beast, he hadn't been able to prevent his eyes from widening. It had given Connor a deep satisfaction, because that widening had been admiration, he was certain of it.

He'd hesitated for only a few seconds before finding Josh and making him suck him off right there in front of Wander. The man had looked at him, one eyebrow raised as if asking what Connor wanted, and when Connor had nodded, Wander had enjoyed the show. It pained Connor to admit it, but the man had been bang on that his presence and that of his men did provide benefits, at least for Connor.

He was lounging on the couch, a soft smile on his face as he listened to the sounds drifting in from the bedroom, where Josh and Indy were snuggling and chatting. They needed that time together, Connor had discovered. It wasn't about sex, though they did enjoy each other from time to time, but rather about simply being together.

He startled when his phone rang, and it took him a little while to even find it, buried under the stack of newspapers he'd been reading. He didn't recognize the number, but the area code was Boston, so he picked up.

"Yeah," he answered.

There was a long pause at the other end of the line, and he was about to hang up when someone finally spoke. "Connor?"

His body froze, an ice-cold chill freezing him to his spot. He would recognize that voice anywhere. "Mom?"

"I'm so glad to hear your voice," his mom said, and despite the warmth in her tone, Connor shivered. He wasn't sure why, but he signaled to Wander something was happening, and the man hurried over and sat down on the couch next to him. Connor tilted his phone enough from his ear so the man could listen in.

"Why are you calling me, mom?" Connor said, and much to his own frustration, his voice wasn't quite steady.

"Jesus, Joseph, and Mary, I've missed ya. It's so good to hear your voice. How have you been?"

Connor's instincts were screaming at him. Why was she calling him out of the blue? And why was she so affectionate and emotional? She hadn't been a bad mom by any standard, but she'd never been overly emotional. She'd been a Fitzpatrick through and through in that sense, rarely letting her feelings get the best of her. No, something was wrong, and the bitter cold in his veins mixed with dread.

"It's good to hear your voice as well, Mom. I've missed you."

It wasn't a lie. He hadn't seen her in many, many years, but he hadn't forgotten about her. She'd made her choices and so had he, but he'd always recognized that it wasn't spite or lack of love for him that had guided her choices. It was more inevitability, what with him taking a stand and her choosing to placate her oh so very dangerous family. She'd done what was necessary to keep herself and his dad safe— at least until he'd passed away—and it was hard to blame her for that.

"I've been good, Mom," he added. "I'm happy."

She let out a muffled sound, a mix between a sob and an exhale. "That's good, my boy. That's good to hear. All I ever wanted was for you to be happy."

There was a strange undertone of truth to that statement, and the dread in his stomach grew. He swallowed back the slight nausea. "Are you okay, Mom?"

It took a while before she answered. "I called to say goodbye."

Goodbye? He clenched his fist so hard his knuckles were white as snow. "What's going on, Mom?"

"I'm calling from a secure place, Connor, and from a burner phone. I know your phone is secure, you know better than to get sloppy. Don't worry, they'll never trace this call."

He didn't like the sound of that at all. "Who?"

"Any of them, take your pick. The family, the boys in blue, those fucking Feds. Connor, is it true, what they said? That you took them down?"

Connor's heart about stopped. Was she talking about him going undercover or about the shooting? "What do you mean, Mom?"

"They say you had something to do with the shooting."

Oh god. He wasn't telling her jack shit. She could promise him up and down this call wasn't recorded, but he wouldn't take the risk. "I don't know what you're talking about."

She laughed, a laugh happier than he'd thought possible. "You have more courage than all of them combined." Then she sobered. "They also said you know the whereabouts of Stephan Moreau. They're pushing me hard to convince you to give him up. I've told them I'd deliver him."

Connor's blood ran as cold as the Arctic. "Mom."

"Oh shush, you. They're morons, fucking chowdaheads, the whole fucking lot. Your uncle George most of all. God, my brother is an idiot. He's blinded by grief and rage."

George was his mother's oldest brother, his late cousin Eric's father—the one who had raped Indy. "Is he in charge now?"

"Not anymore."

"What have you done, Mom?"

He heard her breathe for almost a minute before she spoke again. "I need you to listen to me, Ignatius Sean O'Connor. I regret many things in life, but there's nothing I regret more than not following you when you broke with the family. You did what your dad and I should've done many years ago, but we were too scared. I'm so proud of you."

Connor's eyes started to water, because he could feel it, the finality in her voice. "I love you, Mom. I understood why you did what you did."

A strangled sob traveled through the phone. "Listen carefully now, Connor. Before he died, your father sat down with an attorney and recorded an affidavit, swearing to everything he ever remembered witnessing from the family. He spoke with them for days, and it was all signed and made official. It's admissible in a court of law. I kept it hidden, even after he died, unsure if I wanted to use it." She paused for a moment. "I just handed it over to the DA."

Connor's head spun. His father's testimony would corroborate Indy's story. The trial would no longer depend on Indy's testimony alone. "Mom, that's... Thank you."

"I had to, Connor. We did that more as a safety measure, an insurance policy against the family, you know? It was never meant to be used like this, but I have too much on my conscience already, and when your uncle George kept going on and on about that poor boy..."

"Stephan?" he asked, remembering just in time to use his old name.

"It's horrifying what they did to him, your cousins. I hope they're rotting in hell, both of them. But George was determined to silence him, and I had to do something."

She wasn't talking about his father's testimony any longer, Connor realized. There was an edge to her voice, a chilling coldness. "What did you do, Mom?" he asked all over again.

"Your uncle is dead, let's leave it at that."

Connor fought to hold back a gasp as the truth hit him. "You..." he said, then stopped. He wasn't going to implicate her, not like this.

"If whoever killed him did their job right, they'll never find them, but if they do, you know what will happen."

Connor could hear his own heartbeat in his ears. She'd signed her death warrant if the family or whoever was left ever discovered it had been her. You didn't turn against the family like that. That had consequences, deadly ones. "They'll kill them," he said, and next to him, Wander jerked in shock.

"Yes, but here's the thing, Connor. You're the only one left. My dad, my brothers, their sons, they're all gone. Their wives have all faded into nothing. Nobody is left to lead, you hear what I'm saying? If you stay away, the family is dead. Others may take over, but they won't give a flying shit about George, Eric, Duncan, or any of them. It's no longer personal."

She was right. It was what Connor had hoped to achieve by taking out his uncle and cousins, but he hadn't counted on Eric's father keeping vengeance alive. "Does that mean the contract on Stephan's head will be canceled?"

"Give it a few weeks. George backed that contract, so it'll take time for the news to trickle down that no one's left to honor it."

"What about the lieutenants who are in jail, awaiting trial?"

She laughed again. "The money is gone. All the assets are gone. The cops raided everything, and what was left was seized by George's killer. My guess is, they'll disappear and will never be heard from again."

"Mom..." His throat constricted, understanding what she was telling him.

"One last thing, Connor. There's a lawyer in Boston named Trevon Wilson. If you should hear certain news, wait a while and contact him. Do you understand what I'm saying?"

He did. She'd made a back-up plan in case she got caught. "I love you, Mom," he said again. "Thank you for everything."

"You be happy, Connor," she said, and then she choked up. "You live a long, happy life, you hear me? Don't ever look back."

"Mom..." He lost the battle with his own tears, somehow knowing that he'd never see her again.

"I love you, Connor. You be good now."

And with that, she was gone, leaving him with the same parting words she'd used since he was a little boy. Every day, when she'd put him on the bus, those had been her last words. "You be good now."

He dug his fingernails into his own hands to keep himself from falling apart as the phone dropped out of his hand. Wander snapped something at one of his men, but Connor was too focused on not crumbling to register what. It felt like seconds later that Indy and Josh were running in, then Noah, his heavy footstep always easy to distinguish.

"What the hell happened?"

That was Noah, his voice filled with concern, while Josh dropped to the floor in front of Connor and held him. He allowed it, dropping his head onto Josh's shoulder. He wasn't sure how long he rested like that, his thoughts a tornado of conflicted emotions, before he looked up. Miles had come in as well, both his boys still at work.

"Wander, I need you to leave the room for a few minutes," Connor said, his voice hoarse.

The man had already heard way more than he should have, and with his brother being the DA, Connor wasn't taking any chances. Wander seemed to understand, because he put on his jacket. "I'll do an outside check."

When he was outside, Connor took a steadying breath. This wasn't gonna be easy, especially for Indy. He'd struggled so much already with knowing how many people had suffered and died, and Connor was about to add one more to the list. But he needed to know, they all did.

So Connor told them about the call, relating every detail and word, knowing he could trust them with his life. His family was here for him. Not his family by blood, but his family nonetheless.

"She killed him?" Miles said, his voice rising in pitch.

"The hints she gave were clear. I haven't checked the news, but I'm sure it will be reported, what with the trial starting soon. The Fitzpatricks are still big news."

"She did it to protect you," Noah said slowly.

Connor nodded. "Yah. She said my uncle knew about my involvement in taking the Fitzpatricks down, but I dunno if she meant the raids or the shooting."

He didn't realize it until Indy gasped, the sound crystal clear in the room that had grown eerily quiet. *Oh fuckity fuck.* He'd just admitted he'd been involved in the shooting. Indy had known, and Miles must have suspected, but Noah...

Noah hadn't known. But he did now.

∽

HE'D THOUGHT it had been Josh at first, when he'd first heard about the shooting. Noah remembered staring at that TV screen in the FBI's waiting room in DC, seeing the news report on the shooting in Boston. His first thought had been that it had to be Josh, somehow. But then rational thought had kicked in.

Josh was in a facility, drugged up. Noah had given permission himself since the veteran's psychiatric hospital had decided Josh wasn't in the right frame of mind to consent to treatment anymore. Noah had read the reports, had signed all the papers. Josh had suffered a horrible setback there. So it couldn't have been him.

And yet Connor had just blurted out he'd somehow been involved in that shooting. Noah's head hurt as he tried to piece the puzzle together. The fact that Connor had left so abruptly. Their weird breakup. Josh being in such good spirits when he returned home, with Connor by his side. Indy, who had never wanted to engage in discussions about the shooting, stating he was happy his nightmare was over.

"You knew," he said to Indy, noticing everyone was looking at him.

Indy slowly nodded. "I knew right away when Josh came home."

"How?"

Indy shot Josh a quick look, then said, "Because he was too happy, too confident for a man who was supposed to have had a breakdown like that. Happy with Connor, too, which didn't make sense unless their breakup was fake."

A wave of emotion rolled through Noah. Indy had proved all over again how well he knew Josh, even better than Noah, who'd been his best friend since they were fifteen. "How did I not see it?" he asked Josh. "How did I miss this?"

He didn't say it, but it stung, because he usually was so perceptive.

Josh let go of Connor and cupped Noah's cheeks, kissing him gently on his lips. "You see me differently than Indy does. When you look at me, you still see the bullied high schooler, the insecure gay guy so scared of rejection. You see the soldier who tried so hard to fit in but never really did. And most of all, you see the man you've needed to protect for so long, which you did. You see my weaknesses, Noah, and that's okay. It's who we are and I love you for it. But Indy sees my strengths. He..."

Josh's voice trailed off, and he looked at Indy with such love it took away the sting of his previous words. "He sees who I could be," Josh finished at a whisper. "And so does Connor." He looked back at Noah. "It was Connor's plan, and he asked me, knowing I could pull it off."

Noah had to swallow before he could speak, and Josh let go of his face. "I would've never asked you," he realized. "I would've never put you in that position, too scared you'd choke."

"Don't blame yourself, Noah. You were what I needed for a long, long time. But like you outgrew your need for me and our twisted relationship, so did I. I've grown and changed, and knowing how much Connor believed in me was a huge part of that."

God, he was so right. It hurt to hear it, how much he'd been stuck in his perception of Josh, but it was true. Josh *had* changed, and Noah had never fully adapted his vision of him. "I'm so, so proud of you," he said. "I'm sorry I didn't see it till now, didn't believe in you. But I'll try to do better."

Josh smiled, then leaned in for another soft kiss. "I never held it against you because I know your protective demeanor was born in love for me."

Noah turned his head to face Connor, who'd been watching them with a slight unease. It wasn't because of the affection, Noah realized, but because of the massive ramifications of his unintentional confession. He and Josh had committed a triple murder, and if anyone in this room talked, they could face a long time in prison.

"Did you know?" Noah checked with Miles.

Miles shrugged. "I strongly suspected. I read the FBI file on the shooting and when the ballistic report showed it was a standard issue military sharpshooter rifle, I figured it had to be Josh."

"But you never said anything?" Josh asked with a hint of emotion.

"No. Look, I can't condone vigilante justice, but in this specific case, nothing else would've brought Indy freedom. They could've still ruled the organization had they been imprisoned, so I could live with this outcome, and I'm sure a lot of the investigating agents feel the same way. It's not like innocents were taken out, you know?"

They all nodded in agreement, and Noah's eyes traveled back to Connor, who still sat motionless, his face pale. "Why?" Noah asked. "Why did you do this? You took massive risks."

At first, Noah thought Connor wouldn't answer, but then the man's eyes found Josh and his demeanor changed. "Because I think deep down, I already knew how much Josh loved Indy. Losing Indy would've broken him, and I wanted his happiness more than anything. Plus, I owed Indy."

The last statement didn't make sense to Noah at all, but he let it go. He'd ask Indy about it later, maybe. The bottom line was that what Noah had thought to be a random act by strangers that had resulted in Indy's freedom had been a deliberate plan by Connor and Josh. It filled his chest until the feeling was so big, he could barely contain it.

He dropped off the chair onto the floor on his knees, then clumsily made his way over to where Connor was sitting, who watched his progression with widening eyes. "What the hell are you doing?"

Noah waited until he was close enough, then put his arms around that big chest and leaned in for a strong hug. "I'm thanking you. I owe you everything, Connor. Everything."

It only took a second before Connor returned the hug, squeezing Noah hard. "You don't owe me shit. But you're welcome."

Noah wasn't sure why, but he held on, feeling a tightness in Connor that he couldn't define. It was confirmed when Connor dropped his head onto Noah's shoulder, bringing his mouth close to his ear. "I'm scared."

"For your mom?" Noah asked softly.

He couldn't even begin to comprehend how complicated Connor's relationship with his mother was. He hadn't spoken to her in years, but that didn't mean he didn't love her. And from what Connor had shared about that phone call, she'd saved him. And Indy. Another reason why he owed Connor.

"What if they catch her?"

"Your family?"

"No, the cops. She's right, there's no one left of the family but me. The new lieutenants, they won't care. It's a problem solved for them, probably. It's the cops I'm scared of. If they catch her..."

He didn't finish his words, but he didn't have to. Noah could figure out the rest. Life in prison would not be easy for

Connor's mom, not with her family's legacy. There would be plenty of scores to settle.

"We're here for you," he said, offering all he could.

Connor's head rested on his shoulder in full surrender. "I know. You lot are all the family I'll ever need."

13

Only two more weeks till Christmas, Aaron thought as he watched through the window while a heavy snowfall covered their backyard with a thick, fluffy blanket. Fifteen inches were expected, so his boss had told him to take a snow day and Blake had closed the studio preemptively. Their most recent house-guest had checked out that morning into a new place, and Blake had decided not to accept any new people until after New Year's, so it was just the two of them.

Aaron didn't mind sharing their home with strangers. It was a wonderful thing Blake was doing, offering a safe place to victims of domestic abuse, and Aaron had gotten used to the endless stream of people staying with them.

Shortly after he'd moved back in, Blake had decided to do a little renovation and he'd hired a contractor to create a door between their bedroom and the guest room next door, which had now become their playroom. It was locked from the hallway, only accessible through their bedroom, which ensured total privacy. The contractor had also put some kind of foam on the walls to create sound insulation, and that was a big reassurance for Aaron, who felt free to be himself in that room. It was his safe place, a little piece of heaven.

"Hey, puppy," Blake said, taking a spot behind Aaron and wrapping his arms around him.

Aaron leaned back, breathing in Blake's scent. Just feeling that strong body against his made him happy and content. When he was stressed, touching Blake always helped.

"It's coming down hard," Aaron said.

"Hmm. Vanessa texted me she made it to her new place, so that's good."

Vanessa had been their last guest, and she'd moved away to Rochester to stay out of reach of her soon-to-be ex-husband. "Glad to hear it."

Blake nuzzled his neck. "Burke called me earlier to ask if he could stop by sometime this week. Would that be okay with you?"

Aaron could feel his heart rate spike at even the mention of his name. He'd be the first to admit Burke had behaved well during that Thanksgiving dinner, but that didn't mean his anxiety over Blake's brother and how he'd treat him was gone.

"Of course," he said. "He's your brother."

"Oh my sweet puppy, I'm sorry he's causing you stress," Blake whispered, probably sensing his reaction. "If you want, I can meet him somewhere else, test the waters a bit more."

The brothers had only spoken on the phone a few times since Thanksgiving, Blake busy with a tournament he was organizing in his studio and Burke occupied with looking for work and a place to live. Aaron had been beyond grateful that Blake had never even considered offering Burke a place in their home. He'd have accepted it because it was Blake's brother, but boy, that would've caused him some serious anxiety.

Aaron turned around in Blake's arms. "I don't want to be a hindrance," he said. "I'm happy for you he's back in your life."

Blake's hand scratched his neck in that way that made Aaron want to lick him all over. "You're never a hindrance, puppy. You're the joy of my life. He can wait until you're ready, okay? Besides, I need to see he's changed first myself."

Aaron nodded, then buried his head against Blake's chest, flooded with relief he wouldn't have to face him again just yet. "Thank you."

Blake kissed his head, his hand still scratching his neck, and Aaron melted against him. "You know what I was thinking?" Blake whispered.

"Mmm?"

"We're all alone today... We have the whole house to ourselves. And with that snow, no one will stop by."

Aaron's heart jumped up. "Oh no! What will we do all day?" he said with a laugh.

Blake's laugh rumbled in his chest. "I already turned up the heating in the playroom. Wanna play a little, my sweet puppy?"

Like he even had to ask. Aaron let go of him and shot him a happy smile. "Please."

Blake smacked his ass. "Go get ready for me, pup."

Aaron hurried off to their bedroom, where he had a whole basket full of his puppy gear. He stripped down in seconds, then happily lubed up the gorgeous tail-plug Blake had gotten him a few weeks before. He had multiple ones now, so he could pick whichever he was in the mood for. Today, he picked the newest addition because it had a smaller plug. He still loved that burn as he was filled, and some days he needed to feel it even more, like today.

He put on his puppy mask and secured his knee protectors and the little leather paws for his hands. That way, he could comfortably be on his hands and knees for a while. The floor was hardwood, so it was easy to clean, but Blake had bought several soft blankets and rugs that were washable.

When he was all done, he took his place in the playroom, waiting obediently on hands and knees until his master would appear. He wasn't wearing his collar—that, as always, was up to his master to put on. Aaron shivered in anticipation of that feeling. When that collar snapped close and Master attached the leash, he felt so *owned*, so safe and carefree.

The puppy mask was new. They'd only used it a few times. At first, Aaron hadn't wanted one, thinking it would be too restrictive, and Master had agreed. But then he and Master had watched some videos of puppy play, and Aaron had loved how it had made the puppies more real, and he'd asked if they could try it. They'd gone to a special store to buy one—where Aaron had been red as a beet the whole time—and now he loved it. They still didn't always use it. Master left the choice to Aaron, and he loved that. Today, he wanted to sink deep, so he'd chosen to wear it.

Master usually let him wait for a few minutes so he could clear his head, and this time was no exception. There was no clock in the room, but it had to be ten minutes or so before he showed up. He'd taken his shirt off and was wearing jeans only, his muscles on glorious display. Aaron sat still in eager anticipation while Master kneeled on the floor.

"Come here, puppy," he said, his voice rich and warm.

Aaron crawled over, putting his head against Master's leg. He was rewarded with more neck scratches, and then Master's warm, strong hand caressed his back with long, firm strokes that set his skin on fire. He loved it when Master did that.

"You are such a good puppy. I'm so, so pleased with you," he praised him and Aaron's heart swelled up in his chest. "Can you wag your tail for me?"

He wagged all right, his butt shaking to please his master. Well, the sensation of the plug rubbing inside him wasn't unpleasant either.

"Good puppy," Master said, then smacked him lightly on his butt. "That's enough waggling, pup. I don't want you to get too excited yet."

Aaron obeyed, holding still while Master kept stroking him. "You're so beautiful, so gorgeous. God, look at you..."

He could barely keep still, so happy with that praise that he had to keep himself from bouncing around.

"Okay, let's get your collar on. Can you sit for me, puppy?"

Aaron plopped his butt down on his heels and sat, peering at Master through his mask. He closed his eyes when those hands reached for him, when the leather of his collar was fitted around his neck, then snapped into place. He could cry with the intensity of it, the deep, incomparable rush of being owned.

As usual, Master took him through some exercises that were both fun and a practice in discipline for Aaron. He had to heel as Master walked around the room. Sit while he walked across, then called him. Sit, crawl, wag, he did whatever Master asked, and every time he was praised lavishly.

Time ceased to exist, and his head found that happy place where he almost seemed to leave his own body. A deep joy and contentment took over, the thrill of not having a care in the world. He simply *was,* and it was enough.

"Okay, puppy, rest with me for a bit," Master said as he lowered himself to the floor. Aaron crawled against him, letting his head rest on Master's thigh. "You've been such a good puppy today that you deserve a reward."

Aaron's ears perked up. A reward? Those were usually really good, Master always coming up with something he knew Aaron loved.

"I'm gonna take your puppy mask and your leash off in a second, and I want you to close your eyes and lie on the floor, waiting for me, okay?"

Aaron nodded as a sign he understood, since he wasn't allowed to speak. What did Master have planned if he didn't need his mask?

Seconds later, Master lifted his head off his leg, and Aaron closed his eyes. His mask was taken off, and a snap indicated the leash was taken off his collar as well, though the collar itself remained. Master gently lowered his head to the floor, where it found something soft. A fleece snuggle blanket, Aaron recognized. He stayed still as he heard rustling sounds, his ears straining to interpret them, but it was too hard.

"Open your eyes, puppy."

His eyes flew open, and he scrambled to his hands and knees. Master lay stretched out on a thick, fluffy blanket, completely naked. With his hands folded behind his head, he looked like the epitome of masculine sexiness, and Aaron had to swallow. Please, please tell him he could taste him. He awaited instructions though, not risking losing his reward by being disobedient—though Blake had proved to be a mild master when Aaron got things wrong.

"Your reward is me, puppy, but you can only use your mouth..."

Oh yes. Best reward ever. Before Master could even say another word, Aaron crawled over on hands and knees, trying to decide where to start. He could go straight for the jackpot, but that was so predictable. No, he needed to draw it out, delay the inevitable pleasure.

He plopped down onto his belly at Blake's feet, then sniffed them before he gave a careful lick. Master had washed them, and that showed Aaron he'd planned this. Joy rose in him all over again and he happily sucked in Master's big toe and started licking.

It was a feast, having free roam of Master's body, and Aaron dug in like he was a buffet. He worked his way up from his toes with licks and nibbles and nuzzling till he'd almost reached his groin, then switched to his nipples, which were so wonderful to suck on. Aaron's cock was leaking, but so was Master's, even though Aaron hadn't even touched him there. Master's hands were tight fists, and his muscles quivered as he stayed still.

"Oh god, puppy, you're killing me..." Master moaned. "Your mouth and tongue feel so good."

Wasn't it wonderful how a reward for Aaron was a reward for both of them? Aaron kept up his explorations for a few more minutes, but apparently, Master had reached the end of his patience then, and strong hands grabbed him and flipped him onto his back.

"My turn," Blake growled, and Aaron squealed in delight.

His tail was removed without much finesse and replaced with Blake's cock. He merely swiped some precum off himself and Aaron, guessing correctly that Aaron had lubed his hole in preparation. Aaron pulled up his legs and opened wide.

Blake surged in, slamming home with one big thrust, and Aaron howled. Whereas their play before had been sweet, Blake now took him hard and rough, exactly the way he loved it, and within seconds, he had Aaron coming already. Not that Blake stopped, not even for a second. Hell no, he folded Aaron double and went to town. Aaron took it, greedily sucking in every thrust, every shove, every perfect onslaught on his system.

It was as if the knowledge that no one could hear them fueled their desire, and they were both loud, panting and groaning, bodies smacking together with filthy sounds. Aaron's body raced to catch up with Blake's, aided by Blake's perfect targeting of his prostate.

"You're mine," Blake growled with a possessiveness that made Aaron go weak inside. "Mine." He tensed as he drilled him again. "Mine."

"Yours," Aaron panted. "Always yours."

Seconds away from his second orgasm, with Blake about to come as well, Aaron's heart forced up the words that had been on his mind for weeks.

"Marry me, Blake. Be my owner, my master forever."

14

Josh was worried about Connor. Ever since the phone call with his mother, he'd been withdrawn, moody. Josh understood how hard this was for Connor, or at least he tried to. He wasn't an expert on parental relationships by any standard, not having spoken to his own parents since he enlisted many years ago. And Connor's situation was messy and complicated, and Josh got that.

But it affected him, Connor's mood, the cloud of darkness hanging around him. He'd had flare-ups of his PTSD, more than in the previous months combined, and he struggled with his frustration over that. He wanted to say something to Connor, but he didn't want a repeat of last time, when Lucas had died.

Back then, Josh had worded it poorly, leading Connor to believe he was breaking up with him. He couldn't risk that again, because Connor was hurt, deeply hurt, and Josh wasn't chancing it. No, he needed to figure out a way to say something without Connor taking it the wrong way. He could ask Indy to do it for him, but that seemed wrong. Connor had no issues with Josh's relationship with Indy at all anymore, but this was risking that acceptance. Plus, it didn't feel right to Josh to let Indy do his dirty work.

"You okay?" Noah's voice broke into his thoughts.

Josh looked up from the cupcake batter he'd been stirring mindlessly. "Yes. No." He sighed. "Kinda."

Noah grabbed a seltzer from the fridge, then leaned against the counter. "He's taking it hard, huh?"

Josh felt relieved that Noah knew what was troubling him. "Yeah. I understand, but..."

"It's affecting you."

"Do I say something?" Josh asked, pushing the batter aside. Who cared about stupid cupcakes anyway? It was something he'd started to keep his mind busy. "I'm so scared it'll come off as selfish."

Noah nodded. "I get that, but you're allowed to be a bit selfish here. I can see you struggling."

Josh let out a deep, pent-up sigh. "I am. I could use a scene, but Connor is in no state of mind to do one."

"Is it the pain you need or the sexual release?" Noah asked, and Josh loved him for asking.

"Right now, the pain. We had sex this morning, but I need the endorphins a good session brings."

"Maybe you could call Master Mark and ask for his help?" Noah suggested.

"If I may say something, and please forgive me if I'm horribly out of line," a voice spoke up, startling Josh until he realized it was Wander, who'd been posted by the back door. Josh had completely forgotten about him, used to the man's quiet presence as he was by now.

"Please," Josh said. "Any suggestions?"

As soon as he'd asked it, he realized. How stupid. They had a Dom right here.

"Me," Wander said simply, confirming Josh's line of

thought. "But please, feel free to say no. I'm offering, no obligation at all."

Noah and Josh looked at each other. Josh had to admit the offer was tempting. The man was right here, which made it easy, and they could do it in his own play room. Plus, he'd come to trust Wander and had gotten used to his presence. The man had seen him with Connor often enough to have an idea of what Josh liked and could take.

"I'll need to talk to Connor first," Josh said. He liked the idea, but what if Connor got upset or offended?

"How about you talk to Connor about Wander's offer and I'll talk to him about the rest?" Noah said. "The first is between the two of you, but I think I may be able to help him process his feelings about his mother."

"Oh, I would so appreciate that. Thank you."

Josh hugged Noah tight. He'd just let go of him when his phone rang. When he saw it was Aaron, he debated letting it go, because he really wanted to talk to Connor about Wander, but then he decided not to. He couldn't risk it, not with Aaron, not when their relationship was still fragile. Who knew if Aaron was calling about something important?

"Hey bro," he answered.

"Josh!" Aaron said, his voice bubbling with excitement. "I have wonderful news!"

Josh's face broke open in a smile, because he had a pretty good idea what was coming. There could only be one reason Aaron was this excited, right?

"Did he ask you?" he asked, forcing himself to match Aaron's tone. They hadn't told Aaron and Blake about Connor's mother. How could they, when doing so meant revealing their secret to even more people?

"I asked him. And he said yes."

"You *what*? You asked him? Way to go!" This time, Josh's joy was real. How far Aaron had come, and how wonderful that Blake had overcome his reservations and had accepted. "What happened?"

Aaron launched into a happy tale of how they'd had a play session and had been in bed—Josh smiled when Aaron still couldn't say the word *fuck*—and Aaron had blurted out a proposal.

"How did Blake respond?" Josh asked, fully invested now.

"Well, he came first," Aaron giggled. "The man was seconds away, you know, and so was I. But once we cooled off, he asked me if I was serious, if that was what I wanted. So I told him how much I loved him and that I wanted to be his forever, that I had dreamed of getting married for so long."

He was such a romantic, his little brother, Josh thought affectionately. He and Blake were such a perfect match.

"Blake said he'd always thought he'd never get married but that he'd been thinking a lot about it as well. So he asked if he could think about it for a day, because he didn't want to say yes just to make me happy."

Josh sobered. "That must've been scary for you."

"It was, but not as much as I had expected. I know Blake loves me, so even if he'd said he wasn't ready, it wouldn't have been the end of us. And he's right that he can't do this for me. He has to want it. So he took the time to think it over, and then he told me he'd love nothing more than to make me his officially."

"I'm so happy for you, Aaron. Congratulations. Are you guys talking about a date yet, or do you want to wait a while?"

"About that," Aaron said, and as he continued, Josh's eyes went wide.

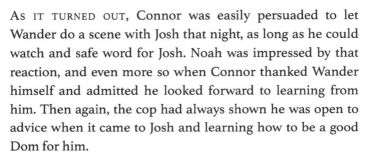

As it turned out, Connor was easily persuaded to let Wander do a scene with Josh that night, as long as he could watch and safe word for Josh. Noah was impressed by that reaction, and even more so when Connor thanked Wander himself and admitted he looked forward to learning from him. Then again, the cop had always shown he was open to advice when it came to Josh and learning how to be a good Dom for him.

Noah figured he could use that session as a good excuse to strike up a conversation when he and Connor were both lounging in the living room. He'd promised Josh he'd try to talk to Connor, and now was as good a time as any. Wander was outside doing a check, leaving one of his men inside, but he was stationed in the kitchen at the moment.

"I'm curious to see what Wander will do to Josh," Noah remarked, causing Connor to look up from his magazine.

"He's got a ton of experience," Connor said. "I'm hoping to learn a thing or two."

"Does it bother you that you can't do a scene yourself?"

Connor cocked his head, seeming to think it over. "Not really. I'm well aware I'm not in a good place right now to do a scene, and Josh needs one. I'm relieved there's a solution, because I was racking my brain trying to figure that out."

"Connor, you could've asked me to take care of that. Not domming Josh," Noah said quickly when Connor looked surprised. "But figuring out a solution. You don't always have to do it all yourself. I'm here to lean on."

Connor blinked slowly, then let out a deep sigh. "I know.

Trust me, I do know. It's just… It's hard. I've been doing things on my own for a long time, and I'm not used to sharing the load just yet."

"I get that, because I've been the same. Just know that I'm here, okay? I know there's stuff you can't share with Josh because it would trigger him, so come find me."

Connor stared at him in a way that made Noah wonder if he really saw him or if he was seeing something else in his mind. Finally, he spoke again. "Have you ever had a feeling something would go wrong? Like a premonition?"

"Yes. Sometimes with patients who'd come in looking okay but my gut said something would go wrong. But sometimes with other stuff as well."

"Were you right, usually?"

Noah had a sinking feeling he knew where this was going. "You getting a bad feeling about your mom?"

"Yah." Connor's voice was barely audible. "The worst."

Noah didn't ask for details since he could figure them out himself. She'd all but confessed to committing murder. A premeditated, cold-blooded murder of her own brother. If the cops caught her… Noah shuddered inwardly at the thought.

"It's been getting stronger and stronger," Connor said. "I think she's gonna die."

What did he say to that, Noah wondered. Denying it was useless. Aside from the fact Noah wasn't God and couldn't predict the future, Connor could very well be right. Noah was never one to counter intuition, and in this case, Connor had every reason to be worried. So, no, denying it was not an option.

"What if she does, Connor?" he asked instead. "How will you cope?"

Connor's head jerked in his direction. The man had

clearly not expected Noah to say that. "No reassurance? You're not even gonna try?"

Noah leaned forward in his chair. "What's the use? We both know her situation is precarious. I've never been one to believe in fairy tales. I'd rather make sure you're strong enough to deal with reality when it hits you. So I'll ask again: if she dies, how will you cope?"

He made sure his voice was warm and kind, even if his words were direct.

"I don't know. I didn't do too well when Lucas died, did I?"

"You gotta give yourself a pass there. That blindsided you."

Connor shook his head. "So did this. I always thought I sucked at expressing my emotions, but it turns out I suck at feeling them, too. I didn't realize I loved Lucas the way I did until they found his body, and I don't think I fully realized how much I love my mom until that call a few days ago."

Oh god, he was so right. Noah hadn't looked at it from that angle, but Connor hit the nail on the head. His relationship with his parents had probably been so complicated, he hadn't even realized there had been a deep love underneath all the frustration.

"You got to tell her in that call," Noah said, remembering Connor's last words to his mom. "If she dies, Connor, she'll go knowing her son loved her and with the knowledge she not only told him she loved him, but showed it too. What she did, it's the ultimate sacrifice to keep you safe."

Connor's eyes welled up, Noah noticed. "That's..." He had to clear his throat before he could continue. "I hadn't looked at it that way."

"It's hard for you because you're so wired to protect others and put them before yourself, but my guess is that you get that from her. She protected you, Connor. She did what she had to do so you'd be safe."

And then it was Noah's turn to choke up, because he still couldn't believe it, what Connor and Josh had done. It was so big, so inconceivably brave and bold. He took a breath to steady himself, Connor looking at him with shaken eyes.

"She did what you did for Indy, you and Josh. God, Connor, don't you see it? She wouldn't want your thanks or your sadness. She'd want your happiness, for you to fully live knowing you'd been given this great gift of a second chance."

Connor stared at him, tears streaming down his face now. Noah let his own fall unashamed. For a while they sat there, their emotions hanging thick in the air. But the silence felt good, comforting, their tears another bridge that connected them.

Then Connor got up from the couch and lowered himself to the floor at Noah's feet, who watched in shock as that strong man put his head on Noah's good leg and wrapped his arms around his waist. "I'm leaning, Noah," he said. "I'm leaning."

And Noah held him for a long, long time, not speaking another word.

The call came later that day through Wander's phone. He took Noah aside. "I asked my brother to call me if there was any news about Connor's mother. He's on the phone, wondering if he should talk to Connor directly?"

Noah could see the truth on his face and his heart sank. "Dammit," he cursed. "I'll take the call and tell him."

Dwyer, the DA, was kind as he relayed the news. Brenda O'Connor, née Fitzpatrick, had been arrested on charges of first-degree murder for the death of George Fitzpatrick, her brother. During questioning, she'd not only confessed to that murder—with details that proved she'd done it—but also to arranging for the sniper attack on her other brother, Brian, and his two sons.

Dwyer's voice turned emotionless as he informed Noah that she'd provided them with the name of the hitman she'd hired—who had turned out to be dead as well. Sadly, once brought back to her holding cell, she'd committed suicide with an unknown substance the detectives hadn't been aware she'd had on her body. She'd died despite attempts to revive her.

By sheer force of will, Noah was able to prevent himself from reacting. God, he was so damn grateful he'd taken the call. In his grief, Connor might've blurted out something and incriminated himself.

"That's a rather shocking turn of events," he said, fighting to keep his voice level.

"It is. They'll do a formal evaluation, but the FBI's preliminary reaction was that this closes their investigation into the shooting in Boston. I'm sure you'll all be relieved to hear that this case can finally be put to rest."

He knows. The way Dwyer worded that suggested he knew the truth. "I'm sure, though it will be a hard hit for Connor to hear his mother was behind it."

Dwyer didn't miss a beat. "He has my deepest sympathies. I hope that in time, the memory of his mother's love for him will comfort him."

There was no doubt anymore. The man knew, and for reasons Noah could only guess at, had decided to pretend he believed the story Brenda O'Connor had told and confessed to.

"Will the trial continue as planned?" Noah asked.

"Yes. The judge has informed us it will start January tenth. I'd advise you to keep your security detail until the trial is over. Wander and I agree that the threat level is low now, but let's stay careful until then."

Noah couldn't agree more. He wouldn't believe it until the whole damn thing was behind them.

"Thank you," he said, meaning it. "We really appreciate it."

"You're welcome. All the best to you and your family."

They held Connor for a long time, Josh, Indy, and Noah, as he raged and wept for his mom. When it got to be too much for Josh, Indy took him to Wander and stood guard with Josh as his safe word while Wander dommed him into subspace. Noah held Connor until he fell asleep, exhausted. And even as his heart broke for Connor, Noah was filled with gratitude they were carrying his grief together.

15

Connor was still tense with pain and grief, even as he hung on the couch like a wrung-out dishcloth, Josh draped on his belly on top of him, silently offering him comfort. They were all hanging out in the living room, watching *Die Hard* for the umpteenth time. Even Wander was watching with them, though his posture was showing he was still alert.

Under any other circumstance, rewatching his favorite Christmas movie would've made Connor happy, but now, his insides felt like a big, gaping hole. Empty. Dark. Stormy.

He'd thought that after losing Lucas, nothing could ever hurt that bad. He'd been wrong. Even though they hadn't been speaking anymore, he'd always known his mom was there if he needed her. And now she was gone. And her last act had been to protect him, to set him free to live. For all her faults and shortcomings, she'd come through in that final moment.

True to her intention, it wasn't guilt that was wrecking him, but rather a bone-deep sadness. She was *gone*. The woman who had given birth to him, who had given him life, was gone forever, another victim of the senseless cycle of violence that had torn his family apart.

He'd cried multiple times since that phone call—and fuck, he'd been grateful Noah had taken it for him—but his body had so much pent-up energy. Connor wasn't sure if it was grief or anger over how she'd died, but he wished he had a way to let it out.

He longed for a hard, long fuck right now. But Josh was not an option. He didn't want to make the same mistake he'd made after Lucas. Plus, Josh was still recovering from his session with Wander, who had flogged him straight into subspace. Even now as they were cuddling, Connor was careful not to touch his back, which was red with beautiful welts.

Maybe... No, he shouldn't even go there. It was a crazy thought, even if Miles had mentioned it on their wedding day. Hell, he hadn't even mentioned it to Josh, feeling too guilty about wanting it in the first place. It wouldn't be fair to Josh, nor to Brad. But damn, the thought of Brad's eager hole taking the Beast... His cock grew even harder just thinking about it, and he rubbed it absentmindedly, slipping a hand between their bodies.

Josh's eyes found Connor's as he noticed. "Babe, you're hard," Josh said.

"It's okay."

"I can..."

"No, you won't." His voice was firm. "I love you, Josh, but you're in no shape right now."

"You can use me."

Brad's voice was timid, but carried over everything and everyone else, even the sound of John McClane almost getting killed in an endless cascade of breaking glass. Miles hit the pause button, and silence descended.

Brad slid off Miles's lap and walked toward them, then kneeled on the floor right next to them, facing Josh. "He can use me, with your permission."

"Brad..." Miles said, his voice hesitant.

Brad swiveled. "You told me you and Charlie were okay with this, that I could offer if I wanted. I want this. You know I do. So I'm telling them, and they can say no if they want."

"He's right," Charlie said. "Brad loves being used. It's why he was so willing to help Miles, even when he didn't know him."

Brad nodded, then met Connor's eyes, who had trouble breathing at even the thought. "I suck at handling emotions. I'm really sorry about your mom, but I don't know what to say, how to make you feel better. But *this*, this I can do to take care of you. You took care of me when Miles was gone. Please, let me take care of you."

Connor didn't know what to say. He pushed himself up and disentangled from Josh, careful not to touch his back. "Babe," he said to him, not sure if it was a plea or a warning.

Josh cocked his head as he made eye contact with Brad. "He's raw, edgy. He won't have the patience to be gentle."

Was he serious? Connor's mouth dropped open. Was Josh seriously considering this?

"I know. I can handle it." Brad's voice was confident.

"Miles, you'll need to be his safe word," Josh said. "You keep an eye on him, and you tell Connor when Brad has reached his limit."

"Babe," Connor said again when Miles nodded his agreement. How could Josh be okay with this? He shouldn't feel pressured, just because Connor needed something he couldn't provide. That wasn't how it worked.

Josh faced him with the sweetest smile on his lips. "You want this, baby. Be honest. When you knew you couldn't fuck me, it's where your mind went. It's why you're still hard, because deep down, this is what you were hoping for."

Hot shame assaulted Connor, and he closed his eyes. He was seriously fucked up for wanting this, and Josh had seen right through him.

"No, don't do that. Don't you dare feel ashamed," Josh said. "I love you. I want you to have this. You'll fuck him, and we'll all watch, and you'll love every second of it. And so will Brad. He needs you as much as you need him right now. Make him feel used, baby, like he's part of us, because he is."

His head spun. Fuck Brad while everyone was watching? His cock was so hard his balls ached. Josh brought their foreheads together, held his shoulders.

"You told me when we met that I did not need to feel ashamed for what I wanted, how I was wired. The same is true for you. This is who you are, baby. You love fucking, you love fucking hard and rough, and dammit, you love doing it in public. You're perfect the way you are."

"I love you." His voice broke.

"I know you do, baby. I want this for you."

He surrendered to the need thundering through his veins. "Okay." He kissed Josh, barely able to hold himself in check, then turned to Brad as they both rose. "Strip," he ordered, his voice low.

"Let's clear the kitchen table," Indy said.

"Maybe put a soft blanket on it?" Charlie suggested.

"I'm gonna step out," Wander said. "You need your privacy now."

Connor heard and saw, but his attention was focused on Brad, who stripped naked in seconds. The boy's cock was hard and more than anything else, that told Connor how much he wanted this, because erections still weren't a guarantee with him.

"Lift your arms, babe." Josh's voice. Connor obeyed, and Josh pulled his shirt off, then made short work of his socks, pants, and underwear. When his cock sprang free, Brad's eyes widened, and he licked his lips.

Connor fisted himself once. "You like my cock?" he heard himself say.

"Fuck, yes, Sir." The 'Sir' rolled off Brad's lips as if he'd done this a thousand times before. "Can I please suck you, Sir?"

He nodded, and seconds later Brad was on his knees in front of him, taking him in, right there in the living room. He hit his throat, but then Brad did something and Connor sank in even deeper, moaning.

Miles had not been exaggerating. Damn, this kid's mouth was wicked, and he sucked cock like a pro. Connor widened his stance. Brad held his mouth and throat open, forming a perfect O with his mouth, and Connor sank in deep, then pulled out. He fucked that wet, hot mouth deeper than he'd ever experienced before.

"Oh, he's good," Indy said.

Connor opened his eyes, suddenly aware everyone was watching. Josh and Indy stood together, Josh holding Indy to his chest. Miles held Charlie, already rubbing himself against Charlie's ass. And Noah was readjusting his cock, undoubtedly enjoying the performance.

Connor smiled despite it all. Fuck, he loved this. A shiver danced along his spine, his balls tingling. "Close," he warned Brad, who kept on sucking as if his life depended on it.

Seconds later, he unloaded, Brad swallowing as much as he could, but some of it was dripping down his chin.

"God, look at him," Charlie said. "Our dirty boy slut,

cum leaking out of his mouth. Doesn't he look beautiful, honey?"

Miles merely groaned, as much in pleasure as in frustration probably.

Brad let go of Connor's cock and sat back on his knees with an eager look, awaiting instructions.

"You want more, boy?"

"Yes, Sir. Please, Sir."

"Kitchen," he pointed.

It was a strange procession of men walking into the kitchen, with Connor and Brad naked and everyone else dressed, but Connor didn't care.

Charlie put a fleece blanket on the kitchen table, and Brad lowered himself onto his stomach, spreading his legs wide and holding on to the edges of the table with both hands. Miles handed Connor a big bottle of lube. Yeah, they were gonna need that.

He stepped close and smacked Brad hard on his ass. He let out a cute little yelp, which amused Connor so much, he slapped him again. "You ready for my cock, boy?"

"Yes, Sir."

"You okay with going bare, or do I need a condom?" Connor looked at Miles as he spoke, though his question was aimed at Brad.

"Bare please, Sir. Wanna feel you fill me up."

"He's negative. We retested last month," Miles confirmed.

Connor nodded, content he wouldn't need a condom. There was no denying the kid was downright eager, and that made him even harder, even after his previous orgasm.

Connor squeezed a good amount of lube onto his fingers. "Open up, boy. I'm gonna start with two fingers, 'cause I wanna see just how hungry your hole is."

"Yes, Sir."

He slid in with ease, Brad pushing back to let him in. "That's a greedy little hole you've got there, boy. You gonna take three fingers for me now?"

"Yes, Sir."

He pulled out, added a third finger. It met some resistance, but Brad relaxed quickly. "Look at you, taking my fat fingers with ease. Oh, you're gonna love my cock, aren't you?"

He scissored his fingers, feeling Brad's canal clinch around him before he bore down again. Brad had to work for it now, little puffs of breath indicating he was breathing through the burn. His inner sleeve tightened, spasmed, then let go, and Connor pushed his fingers in as far as he could.

"Last chance, Brad. Do you want this?" He changed his tone, didn't even want to come close to being his Dom or his daddy or whatever the fuck authority figure would push the man's buttons. He needed to give consent, Brad to Connor, nothing else.

"Yes. Please, Connor. Use me."

A switch flipped in his head. He grabbed his cock, putting some extra lube on it so it was completely slick. Every eye in the room was trained on his Beast, except for Brad, who lay trembling on the table, his head turned to the side.

He lined up, found Brad's hole with the fat head of his cock, and pushed in.

"Ugh..." Brad moaned.

Brad's ass gave way, and he slid in, slow but steady, filling him, breaching him. Everyone was watching how he was fucking. God, he was proud of his cock, proud of his size.

Brad's whimper transitioned into a high-pitched moan. "Oh...fuckfuckfuckfuckfuck..."

He wasn't completely relaxed, but Connor couldn't wait anymore. He pulled back about halfway, then slid back in. Brad's eyes rolled back in his head, and he bit his lip.

"Mmm, what a mighty fine ass you have, boy."

He pulled further out and surged back in with more force. Brad braced himself against the table.

"Yeah, you better hold on to something, boy, 'cause I'm about to unload on your ass. You ready for me? You ready to be pounded?"

"Yes, Sir," Brad managed between clenched teeth. "Bring it, Sir."

Bring it. Connor shivered with adrenaline. Oh, he would bring it, all right.

He pulled out entirely before ramming back in. Brad whinnied, and the whole table moved at least an inch. "Hold that fucking table," Connor snapped.

Hands reached out to steady Brad, others to block the table.

"Come on, Connor, pound that ass," Noah said with a laugh.

He slammed in again, smiling for the first time in days. God, this felt good. He caught Josh's proud look, looking him straight in the eyes as he repeated his move.

Josh's lips curved. "Fuck him harder, baby," he said.

How could he say no to that? A red haze descended as he let loose, truly let loose, for the first time in his life. Even with Josh, he'd always held back a little, but now all bets were off. Brad's body spasmed at some point, from an orgasm Connor guessed, but he didn't care. Nor did he stop when his own orgasm tore through him, unloading his balls with unholy violence. No, he dug his fingers into Brad's hips and fucked him into oblivion.

He threw his head back, roared, and fucked. And fucked. And fucked.

When another orgasm hit, his knees buckled with the sheer force of it, and Noah's hands shot out to steady him. "I've got you, Connor."

He pulled out, finally, his cock sore and his balls aching. He was half out of it still as he spun around and kissed Noah with a bruising force. *Wait, what?* He was kissing Noah? What the fuck?

Noah grinned, touching his lips. "Wrong guy, O'Connor."

He flipped him around again, then pushed him toward Josh, who stood there, smiling. Tenderness flooded him, and he sighed as he took his lips in a soft, sweet kiss. His Josh. What had he ever done to deserve someone like him?

"Let's get you cleaned up, stud," Josh said.

He was led to the bathroom, where Josh cleaned his cock, then offered him boxers.

He shook his head. "No. Too tender."

The fog was dissipating. Had he left Brad there, all by himself? Shit, he was a total asshole.

"They're taking care of him," Josh reassured him. "You fucked him into subspace, a first for him."

"I need to see him, make sure he's okay."

They walked back to the kitchen, Connor still unsteady. Miles was seated on a chair, Brad draped half across his lap with Miles's cock in his mouth, which he was sucking off with glazed eyes. It was more suckling he did, as if the sensation of a cock in his mouth soothed him. Meanwhile, Miles was stroking his back, his ass, murmuring sweet words.

"He's completely out of it," Josh said. "He's in heaven."

"How do we take care of him afterward?" Charlie asked.

"That first time is very disorienting, so you'll need to let him come down gently. Put him in a bath, cuddle, let him come to his senses. After that, the pain is gonna hit hard. He'll need aloe lotion for his ass cheeks, and I have some oils for his hole. You may also want to give him some ibuprofen, and he needs a good night's sleep. He'll be exhausted, tomorrow as well," Josh explained.

"Thank fuck it's break, then," Charlie said. "'Cause I don't think he'll be able to walk tomorrow."

16

O nly a month ago, they'd stood in this gorgeous wintery garden for a wedding, and here they were again, Blake thought. Only this time, it was *his* wedding.

He didn't even feel the cold of the icy wind, his eyes focused on Aaron, who all but danced toward him on Josh's arm. Josh not only gave him away but stood as his best man as well. It was a testament to how hard the brothers had worked to repair their relationship, and for a second, Blake's eyes flitted to Burke, who was present, too. They still had a long way to go, but thank fuck his relationship with Brad had recovered, his younger brother standing next to him as his best man.

Blake's eyes teared up when he saw the pure joy on Aaron's face, so radiant and stunning with the makeup Charlie had done. Blake was wearing a simple black suit, but Aaron, he was the fairest of them all in a pair of tight, black leggings and a long, billowing top with all those bold colors he loved so much. He was breathtaking, and Blake couldn't help but press a soft kiss on his lips when he accepted his hand from Josh.

"Dear friends, what a pleasure it is to be here once again to join these two in marriage," their wedding officiant said—the same one the others had used.

Blake had contacted him, and when he'd explained what he wanted to do, the man hadn't batted an eye. "That sounds wonderful," he'd said. "Count me in."

"We'll keep this short, at the request of the grooms, so I'd like to ask Aaron to say his vows to Blake. Aaron?"

Aaron squeezed Blake's right hand, then took his left one as well as they turned sideways to face each other.

"Dear Blake, I didn't know who I was or what I needed before I met you," Aaron said, his voice soft but clear, a sweet smile on his face. "You showed me what love was, and you set me free to love myself...and then you. You helped me find myself and accept myself, and you always encourage me to be the best version of me I can be. I love you more than anything, and I promise to always love you, obey you, and be loyal to you."

Blake could barely see through his misty eyes, but Aaron's voice signaled his love clearly, his words a beautiful tribute to their dynamics. They hadn't shown each other their vows, and Blake was deeply touched by Aaron's words.

"My sweet puppy, the day you came into my life was the day the sun broke through the clouds. You warmed up my heart and made me believe in love again. I love you beyond words, and there's nothing I value more than your sweet submission to me."

He inhaled as he reached into his pocket for a little surprise Aaron knew nothing about. "Kneel for me, puppy."

Aaron's eyes went big, but he went to his knees in a second. Blake held out the gorgeous new collar he'd bought for him, triggering a chorus of "awws" from those present. It was soft, pink leather of the finest quality and it had a real diamond, as well as a little metal name tag that read "Blake's Puppy."

"Please accept this collar as a token of my love and devotion to you. I promise to always love you, take care of you, protect you, and be worthy of your loyalty and obedience."

He put the collar around Aaron's neck, who tilted his head eagerly, two big tears trailing down his cheeks. Blake made sure the collar was fastened, then attached the leash to it. He'd debated this last part, but he knew how much Aaron loved to be put on a leash, and it said so much about their relationship.

Aaron nuzzled his hand when he was done, then licked it, and with tears in his eyes, Blake gave him the neck scratches he deserved. When he was done, he gave a small tug, and Aaron looked up, his eyes full of love. "Master," he said, and that word had never sounded sweeter.

He rose to his feet, and Blake held on to him tightly as they turned toward the wedding officiant, who beamed at them with a fatherly smile. "By the power vested in me by the state of New York, I pronounce you married. Husbands, you may seal your weddings vows with a kiss."

Whistles rang through the air as Blake took his time kissing his puppy, claiming his mouth until they both ran out of air. "I love you, Aaron Kent," he whispered against Aaron's lips.

Aaron melted against him, his cheeks rosy from the cold. "I'm so happy I'm yours."

"Did you like my little surprise for you?"

Aaron's hand flew up to the collar. "It's so beautiful, Blake. I love it so much."

"Good. I also bought you a ring, by the way, but I figured I'd do this on our wedding day. It seemed fitting."

"You spoil me," Aaron sighed.

Blake kissed him again. "And I love it. Come on, puppy, let's get you and everyone else inside. We're freezing our asses off."

They'd wanted to have a party tent again, but the forecast for another incoming winter storm had changed that plan. They were okay with it, neither of them big party people. Instead, they were having a buffet inside the house and then heading home before the storm hit. Josh had offered to do the food, but Blake had kindly told him they'd have food delivered, knowing how tough a time they'd been through after the death of Connor's mother.

Inside, Josh had laid out the catered buffet on the big kitchen table and it looked delicious. Blake had rented some high-top bar tables and since they hadn't invited any outside guests except for Burke, it was an intimate gathering. Blake had debated inviting Benjamin, but Brad had argued it would only be stressful for him, as he tended to not do well in unfamiliar situations. Plus, he wouldn't have been able to give Aaron his collar during the ceremony, so in a way, it was better. Wander was present, as well as two of his men, but they blended into the background.

Blake couldn't let go of Aaron, even inside. Aaron seemed to feel the same, as he kept close to Blake's side, touching him every so many seconds. Looking at him, Blake wondered why he'd ever even had doubts about marrying him.

"Congratulations to you both," Burke said, extending his hand to Aaron.

Blake was proud of Aaron for accepting the gesture without hesitation. "Thank you. We're happy you could be here today," he said, and only Blake would've detected the slight tremor in his voice because he knew him so well.

Burke then extended his hand to Blake, but he ignored it and pulled him in for a hug. "You're still my brother," he said.

Burke hugged him back with a fierceness bordering on desperation. "I'm so glad to see you happy. And just in case you wondered: you're nothing like him."

When Blake let him go to stare at him, Burke said, "Dad. You're nothing like him. I know you said in the past you weren't sure if you ever wanted to get married because you feared you'd end up like him, but you're nothing like him."

Blake had to swallow, unexpected emotions rising up in him. From the corner of his eye, he caught Brad stepping closer, maybe worried Burke wasn't playing nice. "Thank you. That's the same conclusion I came to when I considered Aaron's proposal."

Burke's eyebrows flew up in surprise. "He asked you?"

Blake smiled. "He did. He got tired of waiting for me to get my shit together."

"He's not the doormat you took him for," Brad snapped at Burke, and Blake loved him for defending Aaron. From the corner of his eye, he caught Wander suppressing a chuckle at that exchange.

Burke's cheeks grew red. "Clearly," he mumbled, at least owning up to his less than favorable impression of Aaron.

"I think we got off on the wrong foot," Aaron said. "Maybe after Christmas, we can have you over some time to talk things through."

Burke blinked a few times, as if he couldn't believe the offer. "I'd appreciate that."

"Good. Let's set that up," Blake said, then kissed Aaron

on his head. "Proud of you, puppy," he whispered when Burke had stepped aside.

Later that night, when it was just the two of them, Blake showed him how proud and grateful he was. He made Aaron howl with pleasure, which he considered quite the fitting achievement for their wedding night.

17

It was the best Christmas ever, Indy decided. First, on Christmas Eve, they'd had Blake and Aaron's wedding, and hadn't that been the sweetest ever? Damn, Indy had totally teared up when Aaron had sunk to his knees and Blake had put that pretty pink collar on him. Those two were so fucking adorable—and that was not a word he'd ever thought he'd use for his once-upon-a-time stern Professor Kent.

More than anything, Indy loved that Blake had felt comfortable enough to show their kink in front of everyone. It must have meant the world to Aaron, and of course, no one had thought it strange. Hell, they had enough kink and fetishes to start a catalog. Compared to all the others, he and Noah were rather tame, Indy realized.

Between the two of them they had no real kinks—aside from their somewhat complicated foursome with Josh and Connor—just a healthy sex life that satisfied them both. Well, him at least. Noah could probably use a little more than what Indy was able to give him. Indy had come a long way since the sex-averse kid he'd been when he met Noah, the skittish boy who hated being even touched. He loved sex now, which in itself was kind of a miracle, really.

Noah didn't use sex anymore to deal with his pain—the fact that his pain had decreased significantly after the second amputation helped—but he still loved to fuck harder and rougher than Indy could take. *Wanted* to take, was more correct. He didn't care for it, appreciated the sweet, tender lovemaking ten times over a hard fuck. But his man felt differently. So Indy could see Noah fucking Brad, too, at some point. Fuck knew Noah had been more than a little interested in watching Connor wreck Brad's ass. Granted, that had been spectacular to watch, also because they'd both gotten so off on it.

Indy had asked himself if he would be jealous if Noah fucked Brad, then decided that he honestly wouldn't be. Not with Brad. Somehow, the fact that the kid craved it so much, loved taking care of people like that, made it different. He'd come twice while being fucked by Connor—and Miles had told Indy afterward that had rarely happened before, only when they double-stuffed him. Hell, Connor had fucked him into subspace.

Yup, they were kinky fuckers, all right. And as they celebrated Christmas together—Blake and Aaron choosing to celebrate alone in lieu of a honeymoon—Indy's heart swelled with pride and love.

They were all together in the living room, the giant Christmas tree blinking with holiday cheer. Josh had baked lemon and chocolate chip Christmas cookies, and the whole house smelled like them.

They'd already exchanged gifts earlier that morning, all small, personal gifts that proved how well they knew each other. Books for Josh, a new chess board for Brad, a gorgeous makeup kit for Charlie. Noah's gift for Indy had been a wedding picture of the four of them on canvas. Indy had cried when he saw it, because they looked so happy. They *were* so happy. He was happier than he'd ever been. He felt it, deep in his soul, as he looked around the room.

Brad and Connor were playing checkers or, more accurately, Brad was destroying Connor in checkers. Connor accepted it with good-humor, asking Brad for tips to improve, which he gladly gave.

Miles, who was chatting with Josh about something to do with gunpowder residue, was getting restless, Indy noted. Probably due another orgasm. Usually Brad would be all over him, but he was too caught up in his checkers game. Charlie, who had been having a quiet conversation with Noah, noticed, too.

He got up, smiled at Noah, then made his way over to Miles. He dropped onto the floor between his legs, and without missing a beat, Charlie's hand disappeared into Miles's pants. Miles kissed him briefly, then continued his talk with Josh as Charlie's hand got busy, the moves suggesting he was jerking Miles off—hard.

How wonderful was it that they could share this with each other? They'd grown used to seeing each other naked, fucking, being sucked off, or in the midst of a spanking session. Hell, he walked around the house himself without his shirt on all the time now, no longer caring everyone could see his scars. This was his family.

It was time for the Christmas present he'd come up with —a little game they'd all love. He'd asked Wander if he was okay with stepping out again, and once he'd explained what the idea was, Wander had said he'd be sorry to miss it, but that he understood. Now, as he caught Indy's signal, he put on his coat and waved at Indy that he was going outside.

"Guys, can I suggest we all move into the kitchen?" Indy

asked. "I have an idea for an epic game you'll all appreciate. Trust me."

There were some surprised faces, but they all got up, except for Charlie and Miles. "Stop jerking Miles off, Charlie. He already came once, he can wait till his next round."

Miles groaned in protest. "You're cock-blocking me!"

"I've got something better in mind. Trust me."

After that, curiosity seemed to get the better of everyone, and they gathered around the kitchen table that had become the focal point of their household.

"What did you have in mind, babe?" Noah asked.

Every face turned Indy's way, and he found himself strangely emotional. "This is a truly special Christmas for me. It's my first one as a married man, but also my first one with all of you together. In September of last year, I met Josh in that store. I saved his life, he keeps telling me." Indy swallowed, his throat tight. "But Noah and Josh saved mine. When I met them, I was broken. Damaged. I'd never known love, and they showed me what love is. They fixed me, made me believe again. They gave me hope."

He brushed away a tear that had managed to slip from his eyes.

"I love them both more than I thought possible. Noah is my rock, my strong protector—even though I could kick his ass if I wanted to."

A ripple of laughter went through his friends.

"Josh, you're my soul mate, my other half. You bring me peace, always. I'm so blessed to have both of you in my life."

The look on both their faces was pure love. His heart felt so full he was afraid it would burst.

"Boston, you showed me what honor is, brotherhood, and I'm a better person for knowing you. I know you're still struggling and grieving, and that's okay. We're here for you."

Josh grabbed Connor's hand, steadied him.

"Miles, Brad, and Charlie, I am so happy you guys are living with us. I know we're all batshit crazy and horny as fuck, but life wouldn't be the same without you. You've helped the four of us find more freedom to be ourselves, no matter what others may think."

His vision went blurry from the tears, and he wiped them off. "When I was a kid and even more as a teen, I dreamed of only one thing: that one day, I would have my own family. I swore would do better. Guys, you're my family. Each and every one of you. I love you all so much."

Chaos ensued as six male bodies wanted to hug him, hold him, then hug each other, and do it all over again. Eyes were moist, soft lips kissed his mouth, warm bodies enveloped him, and he loved every second of it.

"Our family needs to be celebrated today," he continued when everyone had returned to their seats. "We need to celebrate love. Love between lovers, love between friends, love between brothers, and brothers in arms, and family. So, here's what I propose. We all write down one sexual fantasy that we can make happen tonight. Don't put your name on it. If more than four of us can guess who it is, we'll make it come true—if everyone consents."

At first there were some uneasy glances, but then smiles broke through, and eyes started lighting up.

"Oh, this is gonna be fucking awesome," Brad sighed.

"Yeah, like yours is gonna be hard to guess," Charlie teased him.

"No spoilers, people. We'll play this fair." Indy handed out white index cards he'd found in Noah's office drawer. "Use capital letters so I won't recognize the handwriting, start your wish with 'I want,' and speak of yourself in the third person so you don't give too much away. I'll read all of them in random order, and assign them a number. You all get a sheet of paper and when I read a request, write down who you think wrote it. We'll add the score at the end."

Minutes later, Indy had seven index cards in his hands. Oh, this was gonna be an epic night. "Okay, here we go. Write the number and the name of the person who you think wrote this." His eyes teared up as he read the first one. "Number one: I want everyone to either fuck Brad, or come all over him, in a group session."

Everyone started writing, except for Brad, whose mouth dropped open. Interesting, Indy thought. That meant it wasn't Brad. His money was on Charlie or Miles.

"Number two." He giggled as he read it. Oh god, that would be so much fun. "I want Noah and Connor to make out for five minutes, naked, with everyone watching."

Noah and Connor looked at each other, then Noah burst out in a loud belly laugh.

"Someone's got a kinky fantasy," Connor said dryly, but Indy noticed he wasn't protesting. He guessed Noah had put that in, just to piss Connor off.

"Number three," Indy announced as everyone was done writing. "I want everyone to use their hands to make Indy come." It was his own, but he tried to keep his reaction in.

"Indy would have to be okay with that," Noah said, giving away to the others it wasn't him. God, Indy loved him. His first reaction, as always, was to protect Indy.

"As I said, consent comes first. Number four: I want for Noah to fuck Brad."

Interesting. It sounded like something Noah would want, but then who the fuck had put in the fantasy of Noah and Connor making out? It sure as hell wasn't Connor. He wrote down Noah's name, with a question mark.

"Damn, this is harder than I thought," Charlie said.

"I know, right? Next one, number five: I want Connor to be Brad's daddy for an entire day. The kinky daddy kind."

Again, Brad's surprised reaction made it clear that, too, had not come from him. It seemed multiple people wanted something for Brad rather than for themselves. It said so much about how they related to each other.

"Number six: I want us all to fuck Brad until he can't walk anymore, or let him suck us off. You're a popular fantasy, Brad," he added with a smile.

Brad rubbed his eyes, shaking his head. It was so hard for him to realize how loved he was by everyone, how accepted.

"Last one: I want for all of us to help Miles to have so many orgasms he feels truly sated."

It made sense for that one to come from Miles himself, and yet he wasn't the type to request something for himself. No, he'd first look out for Brad, Indy reasoned, so one of the Brad requests had to have come from him. Brad would might choose the daddy thing with Connor, but he, too, would first choose someone else. Miles, probably.

It took a few minutes for everyone to put a definitive name behind each of the requests. Indy kept crossing out names only to replace them with others, not sure if he'd gotten it right.

"Okay, let's hear it. First one, who wanted for us all to fuck Brad or come all over him?"

Charlie raised his hand. "Me. Brad would fucking love it."

Brad beamed. "Sure would. I knew that was you, by the way. I love you, baby."

"Who else got it right?" Indy asked. Four more hands went up. "Brad, you got your wish, but there's more coming for you, pun intended. Number two, a make-out session between Noah and Connor."

"That's me," Josh said, laughing. "Remember when Connor kissed Noah by accident after fucking Brad? Fuck, that was so hot, those two alpha men attacking each other. I want more of that."

Connor shot him an amused look. "Called it," he said. "I debated cheating so I wouldn't have to do it, but that didn't seem fair."

"Yup, called it, too," Noah said. "Kinky little fucker."

Indy counted hands, smiled. "Nice! One alpha make-out session coming. Number three. Right, that's mine."

"Indy!" That was Noah, of course. "Babe, are you sure?"

Indy nodded. "Yeah. I want this, Noah. I've been scared for so long, and I want to share myself with all of you." He swallowed. "Who got it right?"

Aside from his own hand, Miles, Josh, and Connor raised theirs. "Connor?" he asked, surprised.

"It had to be you. No one else here would request that unless they knew for a fact you'd do that. The only one who could have known was Josh, but I already had him for the make-out between me and Noah. It had to be you yourself, Indy. Damn proud of you, kiddo."

Indy smiled. "Thank you. I'm happy it's gonna happen. All right, next one. Noah wants to fuck Brad. Sorry, babe, I didn't need you to confirm that was you."

Brad looked up at Noah, his eyes wide. "Really?" he asked.

"Fuck yes. After seeing Connor pound you, I want in, too. If Indy's okay with it."

"Hell yeah, babe. As long as I can watch your gorgeous ass while you take him."

"Done. Do we need to count hands?" Noah checked.

Every hand went up, except Brad's. "Who did you think it was?" Indy asked him.

"I thought Josh, 'cause he'd okayed Connor fucking me too."

That made sense. It showed how hard it was for Brad to see people liked him, wanted him.

"Who wants Connor to be Brad's daddy for the day? Very hot fantasy, by the way. I do want to demand they do it all at home, in the open."

Connor smiled. "Guilty. Can't wait to boss that boy around for a day. There's gonna be lots of spanking and discipline. And maybe a fucking session or two, three."

Brad jumped off his chair, launching himself at Connor, who caught him with ease. Brad's arms went tight around his neck. "Thank you. I'll be good, I promise."

Connor hugged him back, his face softening. "If you're good, there won't be a reason for me to spank you, now, will there?"

"Good point. I'll be on my brattiest behavior," Brad decided.

Connor gave him a hard kiss, then put him back on his feet, sending him off with a resounding smack on his ass. "Soon, boy."

"We have two left: fucking Brad till he can't walk anymore and helping Miles feel sated for the first time in his life. The two people left are Brad and Miles themselves, so the question is if they are the kind of people who'd request something for themselves, or for someone else..."

The opinions were anonymous on the second option. Brad left his chair for the second time that evening, this time to curl up on Miles's lap. "I love you, Daddy," he sighed. "Thank you for knowing me so well."

"Right back atcha, sweetheart. That's a sweet thing you requested for me."

Indy grinned. "The end result is that we all get what we wanted, unless anyone has objections to any of these requests?"

He looked around the table, saw big smiles, and even a few guys rubbing their hands in anticipation. Oh, this was gonna be so damn hot.

"Since I came up with the whole thing, I think I get to choose the order. We won't get to do all of them tonight, but we can make a start, right? I say we start with Noah and Connor making out. That should get everyone in the mood. Brad, are you up for some serious bottoming?"

Brad nodded, his eyes lighting up. "Hell, yeah. Please. I could use it."

Indy went over the options in his mind. Damn, he was like the director on a porn movie set. "Awesome. Noah, if you're up for it, you can fuck Brad, but we all want to watch."

Noah's smile lit up the room. "Bring it, baby."

"Lesser men would have performance anxiety," Connor said.

"Good thing I know what I'm doing, then."

Indy shook his head. Those two would never change. "Boston, am I right you could use a release as well?"

Connor shot Josh a quick look. "Yeah, but Josh is not bottoming tonight. He's—"

"I know," Indy interrupted him. "I was gonna suggest you use Brad after Noah. You could use the release, and something tells me our little boy slut would be all too happy to take you both."

"Damn right!" Brad shouted, making everyone laugh.

"All right, then. We have a game plan. Let the fun begin!"

~

PERFORMANCE ANXIETY. Noah had huffed at the idea when Connor had teased him with it. But now that it was time to get down to business, so to speak, his stomach swirled. Kissing Connor when he was half out of his mind in a sex-haze, thinking he was kissing Josh, was one thing. Kissing Connor stone-cold sober, buck naked, with everyone watching them... Damn, it was hard. Was he supposed to strip and get all hot and dirty on command?

He shot Connor a careful look from between his eyelashes. The guy looked as uncomfortable as he did, his hands jammed in the pockets of his jeans. And he was supposed to be an exhibitionist, for fuck's sake. Still, he had to have some compassion for the guy, enough to not give him too hard a time.

"You gonna seduce me, O'Connor, or what? I'm growing roots here, man."

Connor's head jerked up as a slow smile spread across his lips. "Don't tell me you need to be romanced, Flint. I ain't in the mood."

"Then fucking kiss me already," Noah grumbled.

The challenge couldn't be clearer, and it took Connor all of one second before he responded. His fist closed around Noah's wrist, giving him a second to brace himself before Connor yanked him close. The consideration in that second, knowing Noah needed that to position his leg correctly, was why Noah allowed himself to be yanked.

Connor's mouth crushed against his, his tongue invading Noah's mouth. He opened up without thinking, and Connor's strong taste enveloped his tongue. This was nothing like the sweet, erotic kisses he exchanged with Indy or the rare French kiss with Josh from before. This was as close to a power struggle as it got—two alphas dueling for supremacy.

Noah pushed back, fought Connor with his tongue, nipping and tasting and swirling. His hands came around Connor's massive frame to circle his waist, then land on his ass. He pulled him close, rubbing his semi against Connor's monster cock. Damn, the guy was already hard as could be.

Noah smiled and squeezed the firm globes of Connor's ass hard, grinding against him. Connor responded with a low, deep moan in his mouth, a sound that shot straight to Noah's balls. Damn, this was *hot*.

Connor tore away his mouth, panting. For two seconds they stared at each other, eyes locked, chests heaving. Then Connor lifted his arms and ripped off his shirt. Noah followed his example. He still had his shirt in his hand when Connor's mouth crashed into his again, that strong tongue demanding entrance. He made him fight for it this time, not giving in until Connor nipped his bottom lip.

Hot desire burned through his veins, firing up every nerve. His fingers found Connor's belt, unbuckled it, followed by his button and zipper. Seconds later, Noah reached inside the man's boxers and closed his fist around that monster cock. It was so damn big he could barely circle it. God, it was fucking beautiful. He fisted it, hard, knowing Connor liked it rough. A deep groan escaped Connor's lips.

Rough hands yanked down Noah's pants, taking care with his stump and prosthesis. Noah stepped out of his jeans and underwear without breaking off the kiss. Connor's hands circled his waist, then dropped lower and pressed Noah's ass. Their cocks ground against each other's, making Noah shiver.

This was so different from Indy, even from Josh. There

was no being careful here, no holding back. It was raw and violent and so fucking hot.

Indy. Was he really okay with this?

Noah retreated, putting his hand against Connor's cheek as he sought Indy. His boy was on Josh's lap, their bodies melted together as only these two could accomplish. Josh's hand was down Indy's pants, jacking him off. Both their eyes were hot and heavy, focused on him and Connor. Indy winked at him, giving Noah the confirmation he needed.

He turned back to Connor and found him watching Indy and Josh with tenderness. The man's love for Josh was a thing of beauty, as was his dedication to their family. Noah owed him. Big time. Connor would deny it up and down, but Noah could never repay him for what he'd done for Indy, for all of them. How could he show him his gratitude and respect?

He kissed Connor's mouth again, softer now, with a tenderness that hadn't been there before. Connor's eyes widened in surprise.

Noah smiled. "Pay attention, O'Connor. This is a one-time thing."

He sank to his knees, ignoring the stab of pain in his stump as he did. He could kneel with his new prosthesis, though it wasn't comfortable. A sharp intake of breath signaled Connor's surprise. Before the man could say anything or react, Noah had closed his mouth around that ginormous cock.

He couldn't suck it in deep, no way. But fucking hell, he'd try to make it good. He circled his right hand around the base, squeezing tight. His left hand trailed between the man's big balls, rolling them in the palm of his hand. He'd watched Josh enough times to know Connor loved that.

"Noah..." Connor moaned, a hint of protest in his voice.

Noah pulled back, moving his jaw up and down a little to relieve the tension. "Your cock deserves to be worshiped, Connor. It's time you realized that."

He sucked it back in as Connor's hands found his head, gentle and tender. Noah tongued his slit, proud when Connor bucked, even though he had to hold that dick tight to prevent the guy from ramming it in too far. Hot damn, it was so fucking big. He tasted strong, bold. Sexy. As dominant as the man himself.

Noah teased him with his teeth, grinning around the cock when Connor bucked again. He brought two hands around the base now, stroking him hard and tight, while sucking as best as he could. It was sloppy, drool pooling everywhere, but what the fuck did he care?

Connor tensed, shivered. "Close," he warned.

Should he swallow? He always did with Indy, but that had to be way less than what Connor was about to unload on him. He still didn't particularly like the taste. No, he wasn't gonna wimp out now. In for a penny, in for the whole motherload.

"Noah!" Connor warned again, but Noah dug in.

"Oh! Unnngghhh!" Connor let out a yell as he came, his massive body shaking with the effort.

Noah's mouth flooded with cum, and he swallowed furiously. Half escaped down his chin before he could swallow again. Two strong hands lifted him up under his arms, setting him back on his feet. Then Connor's mouth was on him again, his tongue swiping his lips and chin to lick off his own cum. Connor dug in, not stopping until they were both out of breath again.

Then Connor pulled away, letting his forehead rest against Noah's, their puffs of breath mingling.

"You're a halfway decent cocksucker, Flint," Connor said.

Noah grinned, then laughed. He loved this man, who had managed to become his best friend. "You're welcome. Now it's time for Brad, 'cause I'm in the mood to fuck hard."

Connor held his wrist as Noah stepped back. "Fuck me instead."

Noah frowned. Had he misheard? "What?" he asked rather stupidly.

"I want you to fuck me."

Connor's face showed he was serious. What the fuck was going on? "Why? No offense, but don't you prefer to top?"

Connor's jaw set. "I do, but right now I want to bottom. For you."

Noah sighed. "If this is some misguided honor thing you feel you have to offer because I sucked you off..."

"It's not. I was gonna offer it to you before you did that."

"Connor, you have to help me, because I don't understand."

Connor's face softened. "I need to feel something. I'm...It hurts, man. Losing my mom, it hurts so fucking much. I need to feel something else, anything else. Please, Noah."

Those last two words hit Noah hard. Had he ever heard this proud, strong man beg like this? He'd been stripped of every dignity he had left because of the pain inside. God, he knew how the man felt.

Noah stepped close again, cupping both of Connor's cheeks. "Okay, Connor. We've got you, okay? Whatever you need. Whoever you need." Connor had choices, and he damn well better realize it.

"I want it to be you. I trust you."

It was a declaration of love more pure than anything Noah had ever heard. He kissed Connor gently. "Okay. Do you want to go to the bedroom, or do you prefer everyone to watch?"

Connor let out an audible sigh, and relief relaxed the stress on his face somewhat. He didn't answer but walked away from Noah, bent himself over the table and held on to the other side with both hands.

Noah nodded. Okay, then. "Hold him tight," he told the others. "And you guys better block this damn table from moving."

He made eye contact with Josh, then Indy. Both sported identical looks of shock, mixed in with pride and maybe a hint of gratitude? Once again, they were taking care of each other. It was in a way Noah had never even dreamed of, but now that the moment had come, it was the most natural thing in the world. He didn't even have to ask Indy for permission, knowing he had it without a doubt. If this was what Connor needed, this was what he would get.

Indy handed Noah a bottle of lube. "I love you," he said.

Noah bent over to kiss him. "I love you, too, baby. You're my everything."

He lubed his cock first, making sure to coat it liberally. Connor wasn't used to bottoming and Noah wasn't exactly small, so he'd do what he could to make it good. It would still hurt, enough to take his mind off everything else, but Noah had no intention of causing more pain than Connor would be able to handle. The guy was a fucking Marine, so it wasn't like he was gonna protest if Noah got too rough. No, this man would suck it up, like he'd sucked up everything these last few years.

"You ready for me, big guy?"

He didn't wait for Connor's answer but pressed on his hole with his lubed index finger. Connor bore down to let him in. Holy fuck, the guy was tight. Noah pushed in all the way, and Connor grunted, tensing for a second before relaxing again. Noah slid his finger in and out until the tight channel around him loosened enough to add a second finger. Again, he didn't wait but slid it all the way in.

Miles, Charlie, and Indy were putting their weight against the table, casually for now, but ready to brace when things got more intense.

"You know, O'Connor, my cock may not be as big as yours or as long as Josh's, but it's thick and strong," Noah said conversationally while pumping his fingers in and out of Connor's hole. "I can already tell you're tight, man, really tight, so I gotta warn you: this is gonna hurt. When my fat cock breaches your hole, you're gonna scream. Like, actually scream."

Connor harrumphed. "Bring it," he snapped.

Noah bit back a smile. The guy was so easy to rile up, but that was exactly what Noah wanted. The more combative Connor would be, the more it would hurt in his own mind—way more than it would in reality.

"I dunno if your ass will even take me, man. It may be too much for you."

Connor turned his head sideways. "If a fucking little elf like Indy can take you, I sure as hell can."

Noah inserted three fingers, not too gently. "Yeah, you keep telling yourself that, big guy. I'm telling you, it's gonna be a tight fit. You're gonna feel like my dick is tearing you in two."

He'd lubed up Connor's ass deeply while prepping him. It would have to do. Fuck, he'd better get this right.

"Get ready, O'Connor. Brace yourself, and for fuck's sake, bear down on me, okay?"

He lined up, planting his foot solidly on the floor. A deep breath filled his lungs with air and his heart with courage. It was what Connor wanted, what he thought he needed. But Noah would take care of him.

He pushed in, halting when the muscles in Connor's sphincter clamped down on him, trying to keep this brutal intruder out. Connor grunted, and Noah waited until he felt him relax, then slid in deeper. It was slow going, Connor's body fighting him, but finally, it allowed him full access. The strong body underneath him was shaking with tremors.

"Harder," Connor said, his voice broken between pants of breath. "Don't fucking hold back, Flint."

Noah closed his eyes, blocking himself from the reaction of the others, who were probably shocked. He would be, too, if he didn't understand Connor so perfectly. Anything was better than that horrible, horrible pain inside. When he'd seen Josh, had registered what had been done to him, how he had been brutalized, Noah had died inside. The hurt had been so intense, so overwhelming, that at times, he hadn't been able to breathe.

But Noah had learned a better way. A hard fuck might bring relief, but only for a short time. The next day, you were right back where you started. Connor thought he needed Noah's brute strength, but what he needed was love. Tenderness.

So Noah leaned over him, covering the man's body with his own as he sank deep inside him. "We love you, Connor," he whispered. "I know that's not what you think you need, but it is."

"I need you to fuck me," Connor managed, his voice tight. "Hard. I need you to hurt me."

Noah set a slow, deep rhythm, their bodies as close as they could be. "You're wrong, Connor. You can't fix hurt by getting hurt. You can only fix it by receiving love."

Connor froze underneath him and Noah stopped, holding perfectly still. "I can't," he said, his voice breaking, and Noah had no trouble interpreting what he meant.

"It's far easier to let us all see you be tough than to see you break down, isn't it? But we're your family, Connor. Allow us to be here for you as much as you've been here for us."

He stayed inside him, sensing Connor's struggle until he spoke again. "Noah..." His voice turned into a sob.

Noah pulled out, and as soon as he did, Connor pushed himself up from the table and turned around to face him, his eyes haunted and broken. "This was supposed to be a hard fuck, damn you."

Connor shoved him, but it wasn't that hard, and Noah saw it coming, which he suspected Connor had done on purpose. He didn't want to make Noah lose balance. He didn't really want to hurt him.

"I know, but we're not willing to let you hurt yourself. We love you, Connor."

Noah saw it happen, the moment the fight left Connor, and that big body lost its tension. "I'm sorry. I didn't... I didn't mean to hurt you."

Noah did what came naturally. He wrapped both his arms around him and pulled him close, not caring they were both buck naked and that everyone was watching. He held him for minutes before Connor let go.

"I'm s—" he started, but Noah pulled his head down and kissed him, because it seemed to him the easiest way to shut him up.

It wasn't a fight this time, but a sweet surrender, Connor allowing Noah to take the lead. The heat ignited again, then burned as their mouths met over and over, until they were rutting against each other.

"God, the two of you are incredible," Josh sighed.

Noah broke off the kiss and found Josh and Indy

watching them, plastered against each other again. "So are you," Noah said, and went back to kissing Connor.

"I still want you to fuck me," Connor groaned.

Noah leaned back and saw a different look in his eyes. Not hurt, not a desire to forget, but want. That, he could support. "Gladly. But I want to see you."

The corner of Connor's mouth pulled up. "You want to make lovey-dovey eyes at me while you're balls deep inside me, Flint?"

Noah kissed him again, just because he could. Connor needed him, even if he didn't realize it himself. Noah could wait. He'd damn well learned patience while waiting for Indy.

"I do. You got a problem with that?" he countered.

The look on Connor's face was priceless, and Noah smiled as he tugged him toward the much more comfortable couch. "You lot can watch, but we need something softer," he declared, pushing Connor onto his back on the couch.

The man allowed it, otherwise Noah would've never managed, but he made use of his compliance and lowered himself on top of him. Connor was still open and Noah was still slick, so he slid right back in with a soft moan.

"You're damn tight and snug around my cock, O'Connor. I gotta say, it feels good."

Connor looked at him as if he was batshit crazy, but then a smile spread across his face. "Glad to be of service. Anything I can do to make it an even better experience?"

Noah lowered his head and nicked his bottom lip with his teeth. "Yeah, shut up and kiss me."

They started out slow and almost sweet, which was unexpected considering the size of their bodies. But then Connor spurred Noah on with little grunts, opening wide.

"Harder," he said in what was more a command than a request.

Of course he would top from the bottom, Noah thought, but he obliged. This was different. This was Connor getting into it, Connor enjoying getting fucked, taking pleasure from it. Noah aimed straight for his prostate, and Connor's copiously leaking Beast was proof it was working.

His hands dug into Connor's hips as Noah pulled back, only to slam back in. Their bodies collided with force now, his balls slapping wet against Connor's flesh. He flexed his hips, drove in again. And again, Connor encouraged him by putting one of those big, meaty hands on his ass and pulling him in. The other went to his dick, which he started jerking off furiously.

Connor came seconds before Noah did, spraying Noah's chest with cum. Noah himself came so hard his breath stopped in his lungs, his balls unloading painfully. He had to blink a few times before his eyes would focus again and he dropped on top of Connor, thanking his lucky stars the man could take his weight. God, he was sweaty all over from the sheer exertion.

Much to his surprise, Connor's hands came around him, and the big man held him, nuzzling Noah's neck with affection. "Thank you," he said. "For knowing what I needed even when I didn't."

Noah grunted, too tired to lift a finger. A few minutes later, Connor lifted him off him, waiting to release him till he'd found his footing. Someone held out a bottle of water, and Noah grabbed it, guzzling it down. Phew, that was better. He'd been parched. Fucking Connor was a workout.

Connor slapped him on his shoulder. "Was that as good for you as it was for me?" he quipped, and Noah's heart surged at seeing how much lighter he was.

"It was, big guy. I'll fuck you anytime you want."

Connor laughed, the sound happier than Noah had heard from him in days.

Noah smiled as he looked around the room. God, he loved these people, each and every one of them. Josh had Indy on his lap, kissing him as if he had no intention of ever letting him go. Miles was sunk low in a reading chair with Brad riding his cock, while Charlie was about to feed his cock to Brad. Meanwhile, Max was gnawing on some bone, looking as happy and blissed out as all the humans in the room.

Indy was right: they were a family. The kinkiest family ever and certainly no angels, but whatever. They had each other's backs. He sighed with contentment as he took another sip of water and leaned against Connor.

Best. Christmas. Ever.

The End

❀

WANT to see Wander get his happily ever after? Start reading No Surrender today!

SIGNED PAPERBACKS AND SWAG

Did you know I have a web store where you can order signed paperbacks of all my books, as well as swag? Head on over to www.noraphoenix.com and check it out!

BOOKS BY NORA PHOENIX

If you loved this book, I have great news for you because I have a LOT of books for you to discover! Most of my books are also available in audio. You can find them all on my website at www.noraphoenix.com/my-books.

Forestville Silver Foxes Series

A brand-new contemporary MM romance series set in the small town of Forestville, Washington, featuring characters in their late forties. These silver foxes think they missed their chance at happiness...until they meet the love of their life, right there in Forestville. A feel good small-town romance series!

The Foster Brothers Series

Growing up in foster care, four boys made a choice to become brothers. Now adults, nothing can come between them...not even when they find love. The Foster Brothers is a contemporary MM romance series with found family, sweet romance, high heat, and a dash of kink.

Irresistible Dragons Series

A spin off series from the Irresistible Omegas that can be read on its own. With dragons, mpreg, stubborn alphas, and a whole new suspense plot, this is one series you don't want to miss.

Forty-Seven Duology

An emotional daddy kink duology with a younger Daddy and an older boy. Also includes first time gay, loads of hurt/comfort, and best friend's father. The third book is a bonus novella featuring secondary characters from the duology.

White House Men Series

An exciting romantic suspense series set in the White House. The perfect combination of sweet and sexy romance, a dash of kink, and a suspense plot that will have you on the edge of your seat. Make sure to read in order.

No Regrets Series

Sexy, kinky, emotional, with a touch of suspense, the No Regrets series is a spin off from the No Shame series that can be read on its own.

Perfect Hands Series

Raw, emotional, both sweet and sexy, with a solid dash of kink, that's the Perfect Hands series. All books can be read as standalones.

No Shame Series

If you love steamy MM romance with a little twist, you'll love the No Shame series. Sexy, emotional, with a bit of suspense and all the feels. Make sure to read in order, as this is a series with a continuing storyline.

Irresistible Omegas Series
An mpreg series with all the heat, epic world building, poly romances (the first two books are MMMM and the rest of the series is MMM), a bit of suspense, and characters that will stay with you for a long time. This is a continuing series, so read in order.

Ignite Series
An epic dystopian sci-fi trilogy where three men have to not only escape a government that wants to jail them for being gay but aliens as well. Slow burn MMM romance.

Stand-Alone Novels
I also have a few stand-alone novels. Some feature kink (like My Professor Daddy or Coming Out on Top), but others are non-kink contemporary romances (like Captain Silver Fox). You'll find something that appeals to you for sure!

Ballsy Boys Series: *Cowritten with K.M. Neuhold*
Sexy porn stars looking for real love! Expect plenty of steam, but all the feels as well. They can be read as stand-alones, but are more fun when read in order.

Kinky Boys Series: *Cowritten with K.M. Neuhold*
More sexy porn stars! This is a spin off series from the Ballsy Boys, set in Las Vegas...and with some kink!

MORE ABOUT NORA PHOENIX

Would you like the long or the short version of my bio?

The short? You got it.

I write steamy gay romance books and I love it. I also love reading books. Books are everything.

How was that?

A little more detail? Gotcha.

I started writing my first stories when I was a teen...on a freaking typewriter. I still have these, and they're adorably romantic. And bad, haha. Fear of failing kept me from following my dream to become a romance author, so you can imagine how proud and ecstatic I am that I finally over-came my fears and self doubt and did it. I adore my genre because I love writing and reading about flawed, strong men who are just a tad broken..but find their happy ever after anyway.

My favorite books to read are pretty much all MM/gay romances as long as it has a happy end. Kink is a plus... Aside from that, I also read a lot of nonfiction and not just books on writing. Popular psychology is a favorite topic of mine and so are self help and sociology.

Hobbies? Ain't nobody got time for that. Just kidding. I love traveling, spending time near the ocean, and hiking. But I love books more.

Come hang out with me in my Facebook Group Nora's Nook where I share previews, sneak peeks, freebies, fun stuff, and much more: https://www.facebook.com/groups/norasnook/

My weekly newsletter gives you updates, exclusive content, and all the inside news on what I'm working on. Sign up here: www.noraphoenix.com/newsletter/

You can also stalk me on
Twitter:
twitter.com/NoraPhoenixMM
Instagram:
www.instagram.com/nora.phoenix/
BookBub:
www.bookbub.com/profile/nora-phoenix

ACKNOWLEDGMENTS

The idea to write a holiday sequel to the No Shame series came to me months ago. Kind of like a Christmas in July moment, really. And man, I loved writing this book. I wrote it while I was going through during a tough period and dealing with a lot of stress and grief, but writing this helped me deal.

These boys will always be special to me. I fell in love with them a little as I created them kind of like a first love. No Filter was the first book I published, and this series became more successful than I could have ever imagined. Even though over a year later, I can see faults and weaknesses, I'm still proud of how I wrote it.

The relationship between Indy and Josh especially was one I struggled with at first. This was my first book, my first series, so how would readers react to something they might as first perceive as cheating? It never was to me, not once they showed me how much they loved each other, and then Noah and Connor were on board as well. I'm still proud for writing it the way it was supposed to be, with all four of them in that messy, complicated relationship.

This book is the continuation of that love, the logical fulfillment, really, with Noah and Connor sharing something as well. They had to, at some point, the chemistry between them too strong not to. But it was never about sex... It's always been about love, in whatever shape or form.

So, we say goodbye to our men once again. For now. But:

I've planned a spin off series where you may see them again, so stay tuned!

A massive thank you to everyone who scrambled to make this release happen after my schedule was thrown off by personal circumstances.

Vicki, I have to mention you first, because in this past year, you've not only become my right hand, but my sanity and my BFF. I know we don't do mushy, but I love you, woman. Also, the new covers are gorgeous.

Kyleen, thank you for your support and flexibility...and for not making me feel guilty. I'm still so fucking proud to be your writing partner.

A big thanks to my loyal beta readers, who managed another fast turnaround on this one. Tania, the other Tania, Vicki, Kyleen, Tanja, Amanda, and Abbie, your feedback was fantastic. Thank you so much.

And last but not least: Jamie, I owe you for editing this one. And the next one, And the ones after that, haha. Thank you for shifting your schedule around to fit this in after my planning went to hell. I promise that one day, I will get my prepositions right. Until then, you'll have to endure hands *in* necks, haha.

Made in United States
Troutdale, OR
10/10/2023